Acclaim for the Anastasia Pollack Crafting Mysteries

Assault with a Deadly Glue Gun

"Crafty cozies don't get any better than this hilarious confection...Anastasia is as deadpan droll as Tina Fey's Liz Lemon, and readers can't help cheering as she copes with caring for a host of colorful characters." – *Publishers Weekly* (starred review)

"Winston has hit a homerun with this hilarious, laugh-until-your-sides-hurt tale." – *Booklist* (starred review)

"A comic tour de force...Lovers of funny mysteries, outrageous puns, self-deprecating humor, and light romance will all find something here." – *ForeWord Magazine* (Book-of-the-Year nominee)

"North Jersey's more mature answer to Stephanie Plum. Funny, gutsy, and determined, Anastasia has a bright future in the planned series." – *Kirkus Reviews*

"...a delightful romp through the halls of who-done-it." – *The Star-Ledger*

"Make way for Lois Winston's promising new series...I'll be eagerly awaiting the next installment in this thoroughly delightful series." – *Mystery Scene Magazine*

"...once you read the first few pages of Lois Winston's first-in-series whodunit, you're hooked for the duration..." – *Bookpage*

"Fans of Stephanie Plum will love Lois Winston's cast of quirky, laughable, and loveable characters...clever and thoroughly entertaining—a must read!" – Brenda Novak, *New York Times* bestselling author

"What a treat—I can't stop laughing! Witty, wise, and delightfully clever, Anastasia is going to be your new best friend. Her mysterious adventures are irresistible—you'll be glued to the page!" – Hank Phillippi Ryan, Agatha, Anthony, and Macavity award-winning author

"You think you've got trouble? Say hello to Anastasia Pollack, who also happens to be queen of the one-liners. Funny, funny, funny—this is a series you don't want to miss!" – Kasey Michaels, *USA Today* bestselling author

Death by Killer Mop Doll
"Anastasia is a crafting Stephanie Plum, surrounded by characters sure to bring chuckles as she careens through the narrative, crossing paths with the detectives assigned to the case and snooping around to solve it." – *Booklist*

"In Winston's droll second cozy featuring crafts magazine editor Anastasia Pollack...readers who relish the offbeat will be rewarded." – *Publishers Weekly*

"...a *30 Rock* vibe...Winston turns out another lighthearted amateur sleuth investigation. Laden with one-liners, Anastasia's second outing points to another successful series in the works." – *Library Journal*

"Winston...plays for plenty of laughs...while letting Anastasia shine as a risk-taking investigator who doesn't always know when to quit." – *Alfred Hitchcock Mystery Magazine*

Revenge of the Crafty Corpse
"Winston peppers the twisty and slightly edgy plot with humor and plenty of craft patterns. Fans of craft mysteries will like this, of course, but so will those who enjoy the smart and snarky humor of Janet Evanovich...." – *Booklist*

"Winston's entertaining third cozy plunges Anastasia into a surprisingly fraught stew of jealousy, greed, and sex...and a Sopranos-worthy lineup of eccentric character..." – *Publishers Weekly*

"A fun addition to a series that keeps getting stronger." – *Romantic Times Magazine*

"Chuckles begin on page one and the steady humor sustains a comedic crafts cozy." – *Library Journal*

"You'll be both surprised and entertained by this terrific mystery." – *Suspense Magazine*

"The book has what a mystery should...It moves along at a good pace...Like all good sleuths, Anastasia pieces together what others don't." – *The Star-Ledger*

Decoupage Can Be Deadly
"*Decoupage Can Be Deadly* is the fourth in the Anastasia Pollock Crafting Mysteries. And the best one yet." – *Suspense Magazine*

"What a great cozy mystery series...Every single character in these books is awesomely quirky and downright hilarious. This series is a true laugh out loud read!" – Books Are Life–Vita Libri

"This adventure grabs you immediately delivering a fast-paced and action-filled drama that doesn't let up from the first page to the surprising conclusion." – Dru's Book Musings

A Stitch to Die For
"If you're a reader who enjoys a well-plotted mystery and loves to laugh, don't miss this one!" – *Suspense Magazine*

Scrapbook of Murder
"This is one of the best books in this delightfully entertaining

whodunit and I hope there are more stories in the future." – Dru's Book Musings

"...a perfect example of what mysteries are all about—deft plotting, believable characters, well-written dialogue, and a satisfying, logical ending. I loved it!" – *Suspense Magazine*

"I read an amazing book recently, y'all — *Scrapbook of Murder* by Lois Winston, #6 in the Anastasia Pollack Crafting Mysteries. All six novels and three novellas in the series are Five Star reads." – Jane Reads

Drop Dead Ornaments

"I always forget how much I love this series until I read the next one and I fall in love all over again..." – Dru's Book Musings

"I love protagonist Anastasia Pollack. She's witty and funny, and she can be sarcastic at times...A great whodunit, with riotous twists and turns, *Drop Dead Ornaments* was a fast, exciting read that really kept me on my toes." – Lisa K's Book Reviews

"...such a fantastic book...I adore Anastasia! She's clever, likable, fun to read about, and easy to root for." – Jane Reads

"I love this series! Not only is Anastasia a 'crime magnet,' she is hilarious and snarky, a delight to read about and a dedicated friend." – Mallory Heart's Cozies

"*Drop Dead Ornaments* is an enjoyable...roller-coaster ride, with secrets and clues tugging the reader this way and that." – Here's How It Happened

"...a light-hearted cozy mystery with lots of energy and definitely lots of action and interaction between characters." – Curling Up By the Fire

Handmade Ho-Ho Homicide

"Merry *Crises*! Lois Winston has brought back Anastasia's delightful first-person narrative of family, friends, dysfunction, and murder, and made it again very entertaining!" – *Kings River Life Magazine*

"Once again, the author knows how to tell a story that immediately grabbed my attention and I couldn't put this book down until the last page was read.... This was one of the best books in this delightfully lovable series." – Dru's Book Musings

"The story had me on the edge of my seat the entire time." – 5 Stars, Baroness Book Trove

"Christmas, cozy mystery, craft, how can I not love this book? Humor, twists and turns, adorable characters make this story truly engaging from the first to the last page." – LibriAmoriMiei

"Take a murder mystery, add some light-hearted humor and weird characters, sprinkle some snow and what you get is *Handmade Ho-Ho Homicide*—a perfect Christmas Cozy read." –5 stars, The Book Decoder

A Sew Deadly Cruise

"*A Sew Deadly Cruise* is absolutely delightful, and I was sorry when it was over. I devoured every word!" – *Suspense* Magazine

"Winston's witty first-person narrative and banter keeps me a fan. Loved it!" –*Kings River Life Magazine*

"The author knows how to tell a story with great aplomb...this was one fantastic whodunit that left me craving for more thrilling adventures." – Dru's Book Musings

"Overall a fun read." – Books a Plenty Book Reviews

"Winston has a gift for writing complicated cozy mysteries while entertaining and educating." – Here's How it Happened

Stitch, Bake, Die!

"Lois Winston has crafted another clever tale...with a backdrop of cross stitching, buttercream, bribery, sabotage, rumors, and murder...vivid descriptions, witty banter, and clever details leading to an exciting and shocking conclusion...a page-turner experience to delight cozy fans." – *Kings River Life Magazine*

"...a crème de la crème of a cozy read." – Brianne's Book Reviews

"...a well-plotted mystery that takes the term 'crafty old lady' to new heights." – Mysteries with Character

"...fast-paced with wacky characters, a fun resort setting, and a puzzling mystery to solve." – Nancy J. Cohen, author of the Bad Hair Day Mysteries

"Lots of action, a bevy of quirky characters, and a treasure trove of secrets add up to another fine read from Lois Winston." – mystery author Maggie Toussaint/Valona Jones

Guilty as Framed

"Engaging and clever!" – *Kings River Life Magazine*
"This is another great entry in the Anastasia Pollack series." – Dru's Book Musings

"Winston not only combines (New) Jersey, well-crafted characters, and tight plotting, but she adds her own interpretation and possible solution to a factual museum art crime." – Debra H. Goldstein, author of the Sarah Blair Mysteries

"Author Lois Winston deftly frames the fast-moving investigation...with a dollop of mother-in-law hijinks, mama drama, home renovation, and doggie intervention." – mystery author Maggie Toussaint/Valona Jones

"Reading a book in this series is like visiting an old friend." – Nancy J. Cohen, author of the Bad Hair Day Mysteries

A Crafty Collage of Crime
"Rich in descriptions of the countryside, and alive with characters you'd recognize if you saw or overheard them, this book held my interest throughout and gave me more than one chuckle. It's a delightful read." – *Kings River Life Magazine*

"Winston imbues her story with current references, an appealing setting, layered plotting, and an unsinkable sleuth. Well done!" – Muddy Rose Reviews

"*A Crafty Collage of Crime* is yet another terrific cozy mystery featuring reluctant amateur sleuth Anastasia Pollack." – Lynn Slaughter, author of *Miss Cue*

"*A Crafty Collage of Crime* was a cute, fun, and entertaining read with independent, engaging, and delightful characters, and the mystery was outstanding, too!" – 5-stars, Novels Alive

Sorry, Knot Sorry
"If you like your mysteries with a healthy dose of humor, Winston delivers." – Kings River Life Magazine

"A twisty-turny plot spiked with red herrings and a double shot of moxie." – award-winning author Maggie Toussaint

"Lois Winston serves up another fast-paced cozy mystery that will have you chuckling through to the end. Add to your beach reads basket for a fun escape!"—Nancy J. Cohen, author of the Bad Hair Day Mysteries

"5 out of 5 stars. Another great read!" Cozy Review Crew

Seams Like the Perfect Crime

"I found myself unable to put the book down until I'd read the very last sentence." 5-Stars, Kim Davis, author of the Cupcake Catering Mysteries and the Aromatherapy Apothecary Mysteries

"Wit and humor abound in this crazy cozy caper as Anastasia and her husband aid their detective friend in hunting down a killer. The tips for memory quilts at the end are a bonus. Highly entertaining!" 5-stars, Nancy J. Cohen, author of the Bad Hair Day Mysteries

"Cozy mystery lovers will devour *Seams Like the Perfect Crime*! It's an entertaining and amusing mystery that shines through with authentic characters." – 5 Stars, Novels Alive

Embroidered Lies and Alibis

"An easy-to-read cozy mystery with engaging characters and a solid whodunit to solve." – Nancy J. Cohen, author of the Bad Hair Days Mysteries

"I read this so quickly, pulled into the story immediately and not stopping until the very end. I'd be remiss if I did not mention the humor sprinkled throughout. Never over done or mad-cap – just the right amount to add to my reading enjoyment." – Sarah Can't Stop Reading Books

"Lois Winston delivers another masterful tale replete with quirky characters, fine dining, crafts, and a first-class mystery." – Maggie Toussaint, award-winning author

"…such a fun and twisty read right from the beginning. I loved how the story balanced humor with suspense." – Bibliophile Foodie

Books by Lois Winston

Anastasia Pollack Crafting Mystery series
Assault with a Deadly Glue Gun
Death by Killer Mop Doll
Revenge of the Crafty Corpse
Decoupage Can Be Deadly
A Stitch to Die For
Scrapbook of Murder
Drop Dead Ornaments
Handmade Ho-Ho Homicide
A Sew Deadly Cruise
Stitch, Bake, Die!
Guilty as Framed
A Crafty Collage of Crimes
Sorry, Knot Sorry
Seams Like the Perfect Crime
Embroidered Lies and Alibis

Anastasia Pollack Crafting Mini-Mysteries
Crewel Intentions
Mosaic Mayhem
Patchwork Peril
Crafty Crimes (all 3 novellas in one volume)

Empty Nest Mystery Series
Definitely Dead
Literally Dead

Romantic Suspense
Love, Lies and a Double Shot of Deception
Lost in Manhattan
Someone to Watch Over Me

Romance and Chick Lit
Talk Gertie to Me
Four Uncles and a Wedding
Hooking Mr. Right
Finding Hope

Novellas and Novelettes
Elementary, My Dear Gertie
Moms in Black, A Mom Squad Caper
Once Upon a Romance
Finding Mr. Right

Children's Chapter Book
The Magic Paintbrush

Nonfiction
Top Ten Reasons Your Novel is Rejected
House Unauthorized
Bake, Love, Write
We'd Rather Be Writing

Crafty Crimes
A Trio of Anastasia Pollack Crafting Mini-Mysteries

LOIS WINSTON

Cover design by L. Winston

ISBN:978-1-940795-07-2

ACKNOWLEDGMENTS

Enormous thanks to Donnell Bell and Irene Peterson for their critiquing and editing skills.

Special thanks to the real Elaine Naiman for her Malice Domestic auction donation which entitled her to be named as a character in *Mosaic Mayhem*.

CONTENTS

CREWEL INTENTION

1

MOSAIC MAYHEM

47

PATCHWORK PERIL

97

CREWEL INTENTIONS

ONE

"Anastasia, I need your help."

I recognized the voice at once. "Erica? You shouldn't be calling me."

"I had to. I don't know where else to turn."

"Hold on." I poked my head out of my cubicle and found the hall empty. Quickly I darted down the corridor to the models' closet, a walk-in storage area where I kept arts and crafts supplies and models from past magazine issues.

Once inside, with the door closed and keeping my voice to a whisper, I said, "Are you crazy? You'll get kicked out of the program." Although I had gleaned my knowledge of WitSec one hundred percent from a now-canceled TV show, I assumed breaking the *No Contact with Anyone from Your Past* rule was definitely grounds for expulsion.

"I've taken precautions."

"What kind of precautions?"

"I'm on a burner phone. No one will know."

Erica Milano, former *American Woman* fashion editor and daughter of crime boss Joey Milano, now lived under an assumed name in an undisclosed city, compliments of Witness Protection. Several months ago, she'd provided a federal prosecutor with evidence against her ex-boyfriend after he tried to kill me. Attempted murder was only one of the many crimes that permanently relocated Ricardo to a federally run establishment with bars on the windows and razor wire landscaping.

In addition, Joey Milano now awaited trial on more than two dozen counts. Thanks to Erica, the Feds had enough information to cripple her father's organization and put him in standard-issue neon-orange jumpsuits for the rest of his life—unless his goons got to her before she testified against him.

"I really shouldn't be talking to you, Erica. For your safety and my own." This call not only put her in jeopardy but might also lead to a couple of Neanderthals with baseball bats showing up at my front door. And they wouldn't be asking directions to Yankee Stadium.

She panicked, her voice trembling as she sniffed back tears. "P...please don't hang up, Anastasia."

I caved. After all, Erica had played a major role in saving my life. I owed her. "What's going on?"

"I need to see you. Can we meet?"

"Is that such a good idea?"

"I'll make sure no one finds out. You're the only person I can trust."

"What about the U.S. Marshals? Aren't they supposed to

protect you?"

"If I tell them what's going on, they'll relocate me."

"So?"

"I can't leave."

"Why not?"

"I've met someone."

Translation: *I have a new boyfriend.* "Won't they relocate him with you?" Again, my source of knowledge was totally television-based.

"He wouldn't be able to move with me."

"Why not?"

"It's complicated."

Isn't everything? I sighed. "I don't think meeting with you is a good idea, Erica."

"I'll pay you."

Bull's eye. Erica knew all about Karl Pollack, my not-so-dearly departed husband, leaving me in debt that rivaled the gross national product of many a small third-world nation. Ricardo had been Karl's bookie, a fact I learned only after Karl dropped dead at a roulette table in Las Vegas when I naively believed he was at a sales meeting in Harrisburg, Pennsylvania. Since then, my life has been reduced to scrounging for whatever additional money I can earn to supplement my paltry craft editor's salary.

"Three thousand dollars," she added.

A sum much too large to pass up, even though I had no clue what she needed from me. Too many bill collectors had me on speed dial, and every day my sons inched closer to college. Right now, I couldn't even afford to send them to the local community college. Hoping I didn't regret whatever I was about to dive blindly into, I said, "Okay, where do you want to meet?"

"First, swear you won't tell anyone."

Was she kidding? "Of course, I won't tell anyone. You shouldn't even be telling me where you are."

A huge heave of relief made its way through the phone line. "Thank you. I knew I could depend on you. I sent you a plane ticket."

"You were pretty sure of yourself. What if I turned you down?"

"I knew you wouldn't."

"And why is that?"

"I saved your life."

My mind flashed on an image of Bing Crosby and Danny Kaye from *White Christmas*, my favorite holiday movie. Throughout the story, Danny Kaye's character manipulates Bing Crosby's character with the same argument. Visions of me plummeting into a similar, non-ending situation with Erica swam around in my head. Would I wind up running to her aid for years to come, risking my life each time she dangled a few thousand dollars in front of me? Probably. Thanks to Karl, I had little choice.

"And what happens once I arrive at this as yet undisclosed location?" I asked.

"I've arranged for a car service to pick you up at the airport."

She hung up before I could say anything else. An hour later the mailroom sent up a FedEx envelope that had arrived for me. Inside I discovered a roundtrip ticket to Pittsburgh and a money order for three thousand dollars.

I stared at both in disbelief. Erica had me booked on a flight leaving out of Newark Liberty the following morning and returning Sunday night. A note indicated that a car service would pick me up at the crack of dawn to drive me to the airport.

~*~

Luckily, Mama had no plans for the weekend and agreed to stay with the boys. I wasn't about to leave two teenagers alone for a couple of days. Not that I didn't trust my sons, but temptation can invade the bodies and brains of even the best of kids. "Where are you going?" she asked.

Mama never met a secret she could keep. Unfortunately, I'm a lousy liar. I turned my back on her, pretending to sort through the mail so she didn't see my face. "Atlanta."

"What in heaven's name for?"

"I'm meeting with a craft book publisher."

"On a weekend? I hope Trimedia is paying you time and a half."

Still keeping my back to her, I said, "It's not for work. It's freelance. And they were nice enough to agree to meet with me over the weekend so I wouldn't have to take any vacation or sick days." Not that I had any left to spare.

At least Erica took my work schedule into consideration when she booked the flights. Whatever the crisis, she seemed confident that I'd be able to solve it over a weekend. Unless she expected me to fly back and forth every weekend from now until she no longer needed my assistance in solving her unknown problem.

TWO

I arrived in Pittsburgh at nine o'clock Saturday morning. A dark-suited driver holding a sign reading *Anastasia* (no last name) waited on the other side of security. Since no other drivers held up signs with names remotely similar to mine, I figured *Anastasia* meant me. I introduced myself, then followed him to his car.

An hour later we drove past a sign that read *Welcome to Oakmont*. We continued for another half mile, making several turns, before he pulled up in front of a small yellow and white two-story clapboard house on a quiet, tree-lined street. Erica waited on the front porch.

At least I think Erica stood on the porch. The woman bore little resemblance to the plus-size, twenty-three-year-old I remembered. If her father's goons had fanned out across the country in search of her, they'd never mistake this woman for Joey Milano's daughter.

Erica had dropped at least thirty pounds and chopped off all but a few inches of her hair, which she'd dyed platinum and wore gelled and spiked. In addition, she'd traded her Donna Karan pantsuits for skinny jeans and a torso hugging Jon Bon Jovi lime green T-shirt that exposed several inches of flesh and a belly button ring.

I finally accepted this stranger as Erica when she ran down the porch steps, threw her arms around me, and started blubbering. "Thank you, thank you so much for coming. You've saved my life."

I hope she didn't mean that literally.

"What's going on?" I asked after she'd calmed down enough to tip the driver and escort me into the house.

"Leave that," she said, indicating my carry-on. "I'll show you to your room later. I made coffee and bought raspberry croissants. Let's talk in the kitchen."

I followed her through a small living room and dining room into a spotless kitchen. All the furnishings looked new. The kitchen appeared recently renovated with granite countertops, stainless-steel appliances, and polished hardwood floors. I thought of my own kitchen with its original circa nineteen-sixties chipped Formica countertops, builder's grade laminated cabinets, and speckled linoleum. I had no idea Witness Protection paid so well.

"You have a lovely home," I said as I took a seat at her glass-topped kitchen table.

She poured two cups of coffee and handed me one before taking the seat opposite me. "Thanks. The renovations took lots of elbow grease. You wouldn't believe what this place looked like when I bought it, but I needed a project to keep my mind off everything that had happened." She paused for a moment, her eyes growing misty as she struggled to continue. "All that I'd given up. My job. Family. Friends."

"I'm sure the situation hasn't been easy." I reached across the table and placed my hand over hers. "It's good to see you."

Her face brightened, and she squeezed my hand. "You, too."

"What should I call you?"

"Erica."

"Really? Isn't that risky?"

"I'm now Erica Miller. WitSec suggests people entering the program keep their first names and the first initial of their last names."

"Why is that?"

She shrugged. "Ease of remembering, I suppose."

I guess I missed that bit of WitSec trivia from the TV show, but the explanation made sense. I couldn't imagine the anxiety involved in Erica having to remember an entirely new back-story of her own life. What if she slipped up? Or forgot something? Keeping her first name provided her with a sense of familiarity and maybe a small amount of comfort.

I polished off a croissant, washing the pastry down with a sip of coffee, then helped myself to another croissant. The time had come to get down to the reason for my visit. "So, what kind of trouble did you get yourself into, Erica Miller?"

"I'm being stalked."

"What?!" I nearly choked on a mouthful of raspberry croissant. "Jeez, Erica! You need to tell your WitSec contact. What do you expect me to do?"

"I told you on the phone, if I tell WitSec, they'll move me, and I can't move."

"Because your new boyfriend can't move. I know. But you didn't tell me why he can't move."

"Darren's divorced. He shares custody of his kids with his ex-wife. WitSec would have to move all of them, and his ex would never agree to that. They're not on the friendliest of terms. Besides, he doesn't know I'm in the program. He can't know. No one can."

And yet, here I am. I tried to reason with her. "You're in danger. What on earth do you expect me to do?"

"I need you to figure out who's stalking me. No one has threatened me. The situation may have nothing to do with my past."

"If no one has threatened you, how do you know you have a stalker? Do you sense someone following you? Have you seen anyone lurking around outside?"

She shook her head. "No and no. But unsigned notes keep showing up. Slipped under my door. On my car windshield. On my desk at work. And gifts sometimes. Left on my porch or at my back door."

"What kind of gifts?"

Erica rose and walked over to the pantry. "I'll show you. I've saved them." She opened the pantry door, pulled down a large box from the top shelf, and returned to the table. I moved the platter of croissants to the kitchen counter to make room for the box that Erica placed on the table between us. She opened the lid and began removing the contents—dozens of pastel envelopes and various small items, all wrapped in white tissue paper and tied with pink satin ribbons.

I unwrapped one of the packages to find a lace edged, white cotton handkerchief embroidered in silk thread with pink tea roses at each corner. I marveled at the museum quality workmanship. "This is quite old," I said. "And definitely handmade."

"There are more." Erica unwrapped a second package. This

one contained a set of crewel-embroidered white linen tea towels, also with a pink rose motif. A third package revealed a pair of ivory gloves, embroidered at the cuffs with rows of tiny pink rosebuds.

"I'm beginning to see a pattern here. Are all the gifts embroidered?"

"Yes, and all the embroideries contain pink roses."

"Are pink roses your favorite flower?"

She nodded.

"Who knows that?"

"Dicky knew, but he probably forgot. He never brought me flowers."

Dicky. AKA Ricardo. I doubt that slime bag forgot anything, but if he'd escaped from prison, the authorities would have notified us. Besides, Ricardo wouldn't send Erica antique embroideries. Such gifts didn't seem like her father's style, either. "What do the cards say?"

Erica opened one of the envelopes and removed the contents, a perforated paper card. Not surprisingly, the cross-stitched design was of a pink rose. I opened the card and read the note written in a flowing script: *My darling, I will be yours forever.* Under that, a hand-drawn rose. No signature, of course. That would be too easy.

"I've received more than two dozen cards so far," said Erica, indicating the stack on the table. "All with different pink rose designs, a flowery sentiment, and no signature, just the drawing."

"When did the notes and gifts start arriving?"

"The first card showed up about three weeks ago, but the frequency is increasing. At first, they arrived every few days. Then I began receiving cards once a day at different times of the day. The gifts began arriving the end of last week. Now sometimes I'll discover more than one card a day and at least one package."

"And you have no idea who might be sending them?"

"None. I thought Darren sent the first card, but when I called to thank him, he denied having sent me a card. Then I realized the handwriting didn't match."

"I'm not surprised. The handwriting is far too feminine for a man."

"You think so?"

"Definitely." However, Erica's not noticing the feminine style of the handwriting didn't surprise me. Her generation used keyboards and keypads to communicate, not pens and paper.

"Your boyfriend wasn't concerned that someone else had sent you a romantic card?"

"He laughed, said I must have a secret admirer, but he wasn't worried because he knew how I felt about him. Since he hadn't sent the first card, I haven't mentioned the subsequent ones or the gifts."

"If you were anyone else, I'd agree with him. There's nothing menacing about these gifts or the cards other than the gift giver chooses to remain anonymous at this point. And that's more mysterious and romantic than menacing."

But Erica wasn't just anyone. She had every right to feel threatened, given that both Ricardo and her father wanted her dead—although I couldn't fathom why either would send her such non-threatening cards and gifts. If Joey Milano knew his daughter's hiding place, she'd be dead by now.

I opened the remaining two packages, a Victorian style needlepoint brooch and a needlepoint eyeglass case, both containing pink rose designs. Then I removed the rest of the cards from their envelopes and spread everything out across the table. "These are quite old."

"How can you tell?"

"From the fabric discoloration and fading and the brittleness of the paper. Are there any shops around here that sell antiques?"

"There's a store on Main Street that sells second-hand furniture. I suppose some might be antiques. The stuff just looks decrepit to me. There's also an outdoor farmer's market at the high school every Saturday morning. Some people sell crafts and flea market type goods. Do you think whoever is leaving these purchased them from one of those places?"

I stood up. "Only one way to find out. Let's go."

~*~

As we walked over to the high school, I learned more about Erica's new life. "Do you like living here?"

"I do. At first this new lifestyle took some getting used to. I've never lived in a small town before, and Oakmont is a really small town by my standards. The population hovers shy of sixty-five hundred. I grew up in The Bronx, surrounded by well over a million neighbors, not to mention an additional seven million in the four other New York City boroughs."

"Do people accept outsiders here?" Erica—at least the old Erica—possessed such low self-esteem. I wondered how her Bronx accent and New York attitude fit into what looked like a town right out of a Norman Rockwell painting.

"The people are wonderful. Everyone is very friendly. The day I moved in, a stream of casserole-carrying neighbors kept showing up at my door. The big problem is returning their friendship. Since I can't talk about my real past, conversation often becomes awkward."

"Don't you have a fictitious background to draw on?"

"I do, but the *new* me is still so unfamiliar to me that the words don't always flow naturally. I'm no actress. Talking about a made-up past is hard work."

"How do you handle those situations when people ask you about your life before you came here?"

"I try as best as I can to turn conversations around to them. I've become a great listener."

"Exactly what have you told people about your past?"

"Not much. Only that I grew up in New Jersey. I figured no one here would know the difference between a Bronx accent and a Jersey accent."

"What about family?"

"I'm an only child whose parents died several years ago, my father from a heart attack, my mother from cancer. I settled in Oakmont because I wanted a slower pace of life."

"And who am I? In case we bump into any of those friendly neighbors of yours."

"You're my Aunt Anna. Anna Miller. You own an art gallery in Manhattan."

I stopped walking and turned to confront her. "You're kidding, right?"

Erica threw her arms up in the air. "I had to make up something, Anastasia. I couldn't say we worked together at a magazine in New Jersey. With your background, I figured you'd know something about art. At least I didn't make you an accountant."

"Have you forgotten that *American Woman* is sold at supermarket check-out lines all across the country? What if someone recognizes me from my editorial photo?"

"Oh. Damn." Her forehead creased with worry lines. "I didn't think about that."

I shook my head, then continued down the sidewalk. Erica fell in step alongside me. "You better hope none of the women of Oakmont read *American Woman*. Or if they do, they're not interested in the crafts section."

"Actually, they do a lot of crafts around here," she mumbled.

"Great."

A few blocks later we arrived at the outdoor market. About three dozen vendor tables set up around the perimeter of the parking lot sold everything from locally grown produce to canned goods to freshly baked pies. Knickknacks and doodads, most likely scavenged from attics and basements, covered about a third of the tables. Of those selling handcrafts, I spied one table of handmade American Girl and Barbie doll clothes, another with personalized pet accessories, and a third with crocheted toilet tissue covers.

We wandered along the aisles, searching for anything embroidered. Finally at one table covered with an assortment of junk, I spied a chicken-scratch-embellished gingham hand towel and several knitted dishrags.

"May I help you find something?" A rotund woman with tight bleached pin curls and a ruddy complexion nearly pounced across the table in her eagerness to part me from my money.

"I collect fabrics embroidered with roses. Do you have any?"

She grabbed a set of salt and pepper shakers from the table and thrust them at me. "How about these? They have roses on them."

"No, thanks. I'm only interested in embroidery."

"This here's red like roses," she said, grabbing the gingham hand towel."

Her face pleaded with me to buy something. I caved. "How much?"

"A dollar?"

I reached for my wallet. Anastasia to the rescue. When I handed her the bill, she seemed relieved I didn't want to haggle her down and expect change.

"That was nice of you," said Erica who had hovered in the background during the transaction.

"What's the unemployment rate around here?"

"High."

"Not surprising." I didn't see any other tables with embroidery, so we decided to walk over to the used furniture shop.

As we left the school parking lot and headed down the sidewalk, a tall, gawky man wearing a Batman T-shirt approached us from the opposite direction.

THREE

When the man lifted his head and spied Erica, his face lit up like a lovesick puppy. His skin flushed pink from his neck to the tips of his ears. He stopped in front of us and tipped the brim of his Pittsburgh Steelers cap. "H...he...hello, M...m...miss M...m...miller."

"Hello, Eldon." Erica turned to me. "This is my Aunt Anna. She's here for a short visit."

Eldon extended both his hands, clasping mine in a limp, sweaty handshake. "M...m...ma'am."

"Nice to meet you, Eldon."

"Eldon and I work together," said Erica.

Erica hadn't told me where she works. Luckily, Eldon seemed in a hurry. After stammering an excuse under his breath, he rushed off without engaging in further conversation.

"Eldon is extremely shy because of his stutter," said Erica.

"He has a crush on you."

"Don't be silly. That's the way Eldon behaves around

everyone."

"Trust me, Erica. Eldon could be your mysterious suitor."

"Oh dear!"

"I thought you'd be happy. If Eldon's leaving you gifts, you don't have to worry about someone connected to Ricardo or the family business."

"True. Only I'd hate to hurt Eldon's feelings." She worried her lower lip. "You really think Eldon is behind the cards and gifts?"

"It's a theory. We'd have to catch him in the act to know for sure."

~*~

Ye Olde Curiosity Shoppe sat in the middle of the block in the Oakmont shopping district, a half-mile stretch of Main Street that ran parallel to the railroad tracks. I wondered how the shop owner paid her rent. The amount of dust coating every horizontal surface led me to believe the store did little business.

Like her flea market counterpart, the proprietor nearly tackled us the moment we entered the shop. "How may I help you ladies today?" Then she recognized Erica. "Hello, dear. And who is this you've brought with you?"

Erica made introductions. "My aunt, Anna Miller. Aunt Anna, this is Tilly Braunfelter. Tilly lives two houses down the street from me."

We exchanged a few pleasantries before Tilly once again eagerly asked if she could assist us.

"I'm looking for rose-embroidered fabrics," I said.

"I once knew a woman who stitched the most magnificent embroideries," said Tilly. "Mostly florals, especially roses."

"Do you have any of her work here?"

"Unfortunately, no. She died over a decade ago." Tilly

addressed Erica. "You probably know her husband. Horace Buckwalter? Such a dear man, and such a shame what's happened to him."

Erica offered me an explanation. "Alzheimer's. He often comes into the library and leafs through travel books and old issues of *National Geographic*."

Did this mean Erica worked at the library? I decided to play it safe by nodding and said, "I see."

Tilly explained further. "Doc says he's probably struggling to hold onto the past by looking at pictures of places where he and his wife once traveled. They worked as missionaries in Africa and Micronesia."

"Doc is Tilly's husband," said Erica, "and the local family physician."

Which explained how Tilly could run a store that did little business. Unlike her desperate counterpart in the high school parking lot, Tilly didn't need to depend on sales of junk for her next meal.

As we were about to leave Ye Olde Curiosity Shoppe, Tilly said, "You might want to try Pins 'n Needles."

"Is that a local needlework shop?" I asked.

"Sort of. Maureen Grover is a seamstress, but she carries some knitting and needlework supplies. More importantly, she and Mrs. Buckwalter were friends. She may have some pieces she'd be willing to sell to you."

~*~

"You work at the library?" I asked as Erica and I followed Tilly's directions to Pins 'n Needles.

"Did I forget to mention that?"

"You did."

"I took a dual major in college, library science and fashion."

"Strange combination."

"Not really." Erica sighed. "I had dreams of working at the Smithsonian as a fashion conservator and researcher. Maybe someday writing books on the history of fashion."

"I'll bet in your wildest dreams you never expected to wind up as a small-town librarian."

"No, but that library science major keeps Erica Miller from having to ask, 'Do you want fries with that?'"

"I'm surprised WitSec allowed you to take a job at a library." Again, all my knowledge about WitSec came from television, but in that cancelled show, none of the people in the program were allowed to work in anything remotely similar to the jobs they held prior to entering the program. Logic told me that would extend to college majors.

She shrugged. "They didn't put up much of an argument. I never worked as a librarian. I started at *American Woman* right out of college."

"You don't think your father will have his goons canvassing libraries?"

"If my father even remembers I studied library science, he'd send those goons to search for me at college and university libraries or research institutions. He'd never think to look for me in a small-town library in Western Pennsylvania."

For her sake, I hoped she was right. From what I heard, Joey Milano wasn't the forgiving and forgetting type. The man popped kneecaps for fun and profit. If he wanted his daughter dead, he wouldn't stop looking until he found and killed her.

~*~

Tilly must have alerted Maureen Grover to our imminent arrival because we found her waiting for us on her front porch when we arrived. "Welcome," she said, holding out her chubby arms and offering us a huge smile. "I understand you ladies are interested in purchasing some embroidery pieces."

"I am," I said. Erica and I introduced ourselves as Maureen led us into her small front parlor, which also served as her shop. Shelves of fabrics and yarn, display cases of embellishments and buttons, and racks of knitting, crochet, and cross stitch pattern books filled the small room.

"I'm afraid I don't have any needlework for sale at the moment," said Maureen, "but I'd be happy to design and stitch a commissioned piece for you. My rates are quite reasonable."

"I'm actually interested in older pieces," I said. "Tilly mentioned that you might have some stitched by a Mrs. Buckwalter."

"Oh, I'd never sell any of those! Mrs. Buckwalter taught me everything I know about sewing and needlecrafts." She motioned to a framed sampler hanging on the wall behind her cash register. "She stitched this as a wedding present when my husband and I were married."

"The workmanship is exquisite," I said, stepping closer to inspect the embroidery, a counted cross stitch excerpt from First Corinthians, along with the bride's and groom's names and wedding date. A border of silk ribbon embroidered daisies surrounded the words. The fabric, a creamy linen, showed signs of acid damage. The framer obviously hadn't used archival quality mounting supplies.

More importantly, the wedding sampler didn't look anything like the gifts Erica had received. Not an embroidered rose in sight.

"She also stitched crewel-embroidered baby samplers for each of my three children," said Maureen, "and cutwork baptism caps."

"I'd love to see them," I said.

"Unfortunately, I no longer have them," said Maureen. "I gave them to my children when they married and started their own families."

"Do you know of anyone in the area who might have antique embroideries to sell?" I asked.

"Let me think." Maureen tapped an index finger against her lower lip and stared at the ceiling for several seconds before finally answering, "Sorry. I can't think of anyone."

~*~

We left Pins 'n Needles and headed back to Erica's house for lunch. On the way, we passed an elderly man dressed in a threadbare black wool suit, far too warm for the balmy last weekend in June, and a navy tie, the bottom point of which stopped several inches above his waist. A scraggly gray beard covered the lower half of his face, and a black fedora sat atop his head. He stopped when Erica addressed him. "Hello, Mr. Buckwalter. Are you going to the library?"

He thought for a moment, scratching his cheek, then shook his head. "Ghana. For a year."

Erica patted his arm. "Have a nice trip."

"We do missionary work, me and the missus."

"Yes, I know."

"He'll wind up at the library," said Erica after Mr. Buckwalter continued down the street. "He always does."

"He wanders around town on his own? Doesn't anyone take care of him?"

"His daughters stop by several times a day, bringing meals, doing his laundry, cleaning the house, driving him to doctor appointments. Beyond that, the entire town watches out for him, seeing that he gets home when he becomes confused and forgets where he lives. Since he no longer owns a car, he can't go too far. His family doesn't worry that he'll wind up in Cleveland or Philadelphia."

We had arrived back at Erica's house. At the edge of her walkway, we both stopped short. A large white porcelain cachepot filled with pink tea roses sat on her top step.

FOUR

"He's never left anything besides embroidery before," said Erica, her voice barely audible.

"Eldon might have dropped the flowers off earlier. When we saw him, he was coming from the direction of your house."

She pondered this for a moment. "I think you're wrong about Eldon. Even if he does have a crush on me, he's not a roses and embroidery kind of guy."

"What kind of guy is he?"

"A geek. The kind who collects comic books and speaks Klingon. He's spending his vacation this year at Dragon Con in Atlanta."

"Which means he lives in a fantasy world. I really think he's your secret admirer, Erica." The thought filled me with relief, edging out the dread that settled in the pit of my stomach whenever I considered the alternative—tangling with some of Joey Milano's paid assassins.

We made our way down the walk and climbed the four steps

to the front porch. I stooped to pick up the small white florist's envelope propped against the cachepot and handed it to Erica.

Her fingers trembled as she opened the flap and slid out the card. Then she let loose a huge sigh of relief and began to laugh. "Definitely not Eldon."

I grabbed the card from her and read:

Darling,
I remembered you once said roses were your favorite flower. Rather than a bouquet, I thought you'd like to plant these in your garden, so they'll grow along with our love.

Happy anniversary,
Darren

"Anniversary?"

"We met three months ago today," said Erica, a huge grin planted on her face. "I can't believe he remembered!"

Definitely a step up from Ricardo. That man didn't have a thoughtful bone in his body. "He seems like quite a guy," I said as we entered the house. Although I worried that Erica might be jumping into a relationship too soon, given that Ricardo had been her one and only boyfriend prior to Darren.

"I can't wait for you to meet him, Anastasia. I know you'll love him."

Funny, I remember her saying something similar about *Dicky* AKA Ricardo. And look how that ended. But I bit my tongue and hoped for the best. After all she'd lived through, Erica deserved a heaping dose of good luck.

However, I nixed meeting Darren. "Coming here once is dangerous, Erica. I can't return, and you can't visit me. What happens if you become Mrs. Darren What's-His-Name?"

"Applegate. Darren Applegate."

"Once he meets me, he'll expect me at the wedding, not to mention various future family events. He'll wonder why I never invite you to visit me. Why we never even talk on the phone. How are you going to explain that I've dropped off the face of the earth?"

"But I already told him you were coming this weekend. He's planning to take us both out to dinner tonight."

"That was foolish."

Her eyes welled up with tears. "You have no idea how lonely and depressed I get! I gave up so much. I miss you and Cloris and everyone else at work. And my cousins. Gina and I were like sisters, and I'll never see her again."

She collapsed onto the sofa, buried her head in her hands, and bawled. I let her cry until she'd exhausted all her tears. "Why me?" she whispered as she rubbed her runny nose on her sleeve.

I patted her shoulder. "I've asked myself that same question nearly every day since Karl died. And the only answer I can come up with is that no one ever guaranteed us life would be fair."

"At least you still have your sons and your mom. I have no one."

"For the weekend you have me, and if Darren is the keeper he seems, you'll soon be part of a new family. One without mob connections."

"I hate my father," she said.

"I'm sure he's not feeling too kindly toward you these days. That's why we have to be careful. No more contact after this, Erica. I don't want to be responsible for luring a hit man to your doorstep."

Her face filed with panic. "But what if we don't figure out who the mystery rose guy is by the time you leave tomorrow? What if he really is someone my father or Dicky sent?"

"And he's doing what? Playing with you? That makes no sense. If someone from your past wanted you dead and he'd found you, you'd be dead already."

"That's blunt."

"A fact is a fact. You're a Mafia princess, Erica. You come from a family of contract killers. They don't toy with their victims. They'd aim, shoot, and hightail it out of Oakmont before anyone knew what happened. Whoever your mystery man is, he's someone not connected to your family."

"How can you be sure?"

"Use your head. You grew up in the mob. You know how these guys operate."

She sighed. "I suppose you're right."

"I know I'm right. However, that doesn't mean whoever this mystery man is, he's not dangerous, just potentially a different kind of dangerous."

Although a mysterious suitor held an element of charm, the situation also might lead to Norman Bates type creepiness. If Erica rebuffed the man, would he turn psycho on her?

"So what do we do now?"

"We need to find out if there are other needlework shops relatively close to Oakmont."

Erica shrugged. "I don't do needlework. If they exist, they're off my radar."

"Where's your computer?"

She led me upstairs to a small bedroom she used as an office, then left to make us some lunch. I sat down at the desk, fired up her laptop and began a search, not expecting to find much. Most independent needlework shops folded years ago, forced out of business by the big box stores and the craft chains, many of which no longer carried much in the way of needlework supplies. Nowadays, about the only place to buy cross stitch, needlepoint, and embroidery products was online or through a few remaining mail order catalogs.

The majority of hits that popped up from my Google search brought me to machine embroidery shops, the kind that personalize baseball caps, T-shirts, and tote bags. However, I did find a needlepoint shop located less than ten miles from Oakmont and two others more than an hour's drive in opposite directions. Discounting those as too much of a stretch for a lovelorn stalker, I printed out directions to the first shop, then joined Erica in the kitchen.

~*~

When we finished our lunch, we set off in Erica's red Prius for Shadyside, a Pittsburgh neighborhood not far from the campuses of both Carnegie Mellon and the University of Pittsburgh.

I remembered Erica driving a gas-guzzling Cadillac and wondered if that car had belonged to her father. Not to stereotype, but I didn't think many Caddie drivers cared enough about the environment to trade their wheels in for a hybrid. However, given Erica's earlier breakdown, I decided against bringing up the subject.

"This is where I met Darren," she said as we drove past the University of Pittsburgh. "He's an admissions counselor at Pitt."

A definite improvement over a Mafia loan shark. I was beginning to feel better and better about Darren Applegate. "Are you taking courses?"

"I'm auditing a few classes to see if I want to go back to school. With all the government cutbacks, who knows how long I'll have a job at the library?"

"Given the uncertainty of your job, I'm surprised you bought a house and put so much into renovations. Not to mention bribing me with three thousand dollars to help you find your stalker."

Erica came to a stop at a red light and turned to face me. "The job isn't about money, Anastasia. I have more money than I'll ever need."

I stared at her, waiting for an explanation. Finally, she grinned, then said. "Remember that scene in *The Sopranos* when Carmella helped herself to some of Tony's stash, then opened up accounts in her name at several banks?"

"Weren't you a little young for *The Sopranos*?"

"I caught the show in reruns."

"Are you telling me you stole from your father?"

"Damn right. A hell of a lot more than Carmella took from Tony, too."

"I'm betting WitSec doesn't know."

"Of course not. You think I'm crazy?"

Yes, I did, but I kept my mouth shut. Joey Milano had more than one reason for wanting his daughter dead. I'm guessing from Erica's *more money than I'll ever need* comment, he probably had at least a million reasons.

Even though I doubted her stalker had any connection to Ricardo or her father, Joey had probably put a hit out on Erica the moment he discovered both his money and his daughter missing. Hopefully, his gun-toting muscle men would never find their way to Oakmont, Pennsylvania.

Two minutes later, Erica pulled into a parking space on Walnut Street, Shadyside's upscale commercial district. "The shop should be somewhere on the next block," she said.

We exited the car and began walking. In the middle of the next block we found Needle Me, a needlepoint shop featuring hand-painted canvases and a finishing service.

Upon entering the store, I glanced around. Needlepoint canvases, both stitched and unstitched, covered most of the walls to my left and right. A framed needlepoint sign hanging on the back wall behind the counter advised of a custom design service specializing in needlepoint portraits of your home or pets.

A second framed needlepoint sign listed the prices for various forms of finishing. My eyes nearly bugged out of my head as I read. Finishing a needlepoint dollhouse carpet cost eighty-five dollars! And that didn't include the price of the needlepoint canvas or yarn.

Maybe I should quit my editorial job and open a needlepoint shop. A glance at the canvas prices told me I should at least consider exploring the possibility of selling hand-painted canvases.

Unlike the women in Oakmont, the two saleswomen working in this shop ignored us as we walked around. Both were too busy waiting on paying customers eager to hand over their gold cards for hundreds of dollars' worth of canvas and yarn.

"I don't see anything similar to my pieces," said Erica as we studied the merchandise.

"I didn't expect to."

"Then why are we here?"

Before I could answer her, a salesperson finally approached us. "May I help you?"

"Yes," I said. "I collect old embroidery pieces. Would you

know where I might find some?"

"This is a needlepoint shop," she said. "We don't handle embroidery."

"I see that, but I thought you might know—"

She waved in the direction of the front door. "You can try a few of the antique shops in the area." Then she abruptly walked away to wait on another customer.

"Rude, wasn't she?" asked Erica after we exited the shop. "She should only know who my father is."

"Erica!"

"Just kidding." She laughed. "You should see the look on your face."

"You should remember who you are now and not breathe a word about your past. Especially in public."

She sighed. "You're right. I'm sorry."

She rooted in her purse for her iPhone and searched for the location of antiques shops in Shadyside. "I found five. Two on Walnut and three on a couple of the side streets."

We headed for the closest one.

~*~

An unsuccessful hour and a half later, after stopping in a café for lattes, we settled into the car to head back to Erica's house. One of the shops sold antique samplers stitched by schoolgirls in the nineteenth century. The rest had no needlework at all, and the shop owners knew of no one with a penchant for embroidering roses.

We arrived back in Oakmont to find two people sitting in a black Range Rover with New York plates, parked directly across the street from Erica's house.

FIVE

Erica noticed the car first. After a short gasp, she continued to drive down the street instead of pulling into her driveway. Neither of us turned to look at the occupants in the Range Rover, but after we passed them, Erica glanced up at her rearview mirror.

"Do you recognize them?" I asked.

She shook her head. "Hard to tell. Two men. They're both wearing sunglasses and ball caps."

"Would your father's goons be stupid enough to show up in a car with New York license plates?"

"Who knows? I'm not taking any chances. We'll park on the next block, cut through my neighbor's property, and enter my house through the back door."

"Has this happened before?" I asked as we darted through the yard of the house that backed up onto her property.

"No."

Her answer scared the caca out of me. Erica had called me on a burner phone, but what if someone had bugged my phone and intercepted her call?

Ricardo had confessed, sparing me the need to testify in court. He then ratted out Erica's father, hoping for a reduced sentence, but the prosecutor refused to cut him a deal. I guess he had more than enough evidence on Joey Milano from his daughter.

With Ricardo behind bars, I hadn't worried about my own safety. No one suggested otherwise or offered the option of Witness Protection to me. But what if Joey Milano had been keeping tabs on me all along, hoping I'd eventually lead him to Erica? Which I may have done by agreeing to come here. "You need to contact your WitSec handler at once," I said.

"I can't. I'll lose Darren."

"You're going to lose a lot more than a boyfriend if you don't." And what about me? If the guys in the Range Rover planned to carry out a hit on Erica, they weren't going to leave me around as a witness.

"Grab a change of clothes," I said after she unlocked the back door and we slipped into the house. "We're not staying here."

"Where will we go?"

"A hotel for now."

She raced upstairs.

"Don't turn on any lights, and keep away from the windows," I called after her.

My overnight bag still sat at the foot of the stairs. I grabbed the strap and positioned myself off to the side of the living room window, giving me a view of the street without risk of being seen by anyone outside.

The minutes ticked by. *What was taking her so long?* "Hurry up!" I yelled. My life was flashing before my eyes, and I didn't like the ending.

"I am!"

A minute later I heard the toilet flush. Finally, she ran back downstairs, a gym bag looped over her shoulder—just as a blue minivan pulled into the driveway of the house across the street.

The two men stepped from the Range Rover. One appeared to be in his forties, the other in his seventies. Neither carried a gun. They headed for the minivan as the side door slid open. Two young boys jumped out and raced into the men's arms.

"False alarm." I slid down the wall and collapsed onto the floor. Maybe by next Tuesday, if I were lucky, my blood pressure would return from the stratosphere.

Erica stared out the window at the happy family reunion. "I need a drink."

"Make mine a triple."

After a few drinks, Erica and I calmed down sufficiently not to arouse any suspicions regarding our harrowing, non-life-threatening escapade. Still, I'd feel much safer once my plane departed from the Pittsburgh airport the next evening, even though, once back in New Jersey, I now needed to make sure no electronic bugs lurked in either my house or my office. The thought of Joey Milano or one of his goons eavesdropping on my life left me totally freaked out. Been there, done that. And once had been one time too many.

~*~

Erica's doorbell rang at six-thirty. She ran to the door and swung it open. "Darren—" In a split second her voice shifted from excited to horrified. "Where did you get those?"

As he stepped into the living room, I saw what had rattled her. In his hands he held a pale pink envelope and a small package wrapped in white tissue paper and tied with a pink ribbon.

"They were sitting at your door," he said. He leaned over to peck her cheek. "Do I have competition?"

Erica recovered quickly, snatching the package and envelope from him. She forced a laugh. "Of course not. I forgot. They're from my next-door neighbor. I guess she left them while we were in the backyard earlier."

"Why is your next-door neighbor leaving you gifts?"

"It's...uhm...a...a thank-you for some research I did for her at the library. For her mother. For a nursing home. She needs to find a nursing home for her mother."

Poor Erica. She'd stroke out if we didn't unmask her love-struck mystery man before I left tomorrow. I needed to set a trap to catch Eldon in the act.

Right now, though, I knew I'd better empty my brain of anything remotely connected to love-struck geeks, stalkers, and mob hit men until after my dinner with Erica and her boyfriend. I had an evening of lies ahead of me, thanks to Erica, and needed to concentrate on not screwing up.

Darren Applegate was not at all what I had pictured, given Erica's only other romance, the gorilla-like Ricardo. At least ten years older than Erica, Darren shared no physical traits with apes and bore a striking resemblance to Jude Law, minus the receding hairline.

"I get that a lot," he said when I mentioned the likeness. "Wish I earned his kind of money."

After a few more pleasantries, the three of us left the house and piled into Darren's SUV to head to the restaurant. Darren began peppering me with questions the moment he pulled out of Erica's driveway. "Erica tells me you own an art gallery in Manhattan, but she hasn't said much more about you, Anastasia. I didn't even know she had any family until she mentioned your visit this weekend."

"I'm all the family she has." Then I used Erica's tactic and turned the conversation around to him. "I understand you have children, Darren. Tell me about them."

Didn't all parents love to brag about their kids? Darren didn't disappoint. Over the twenty-minute drive back to Shadyside, I heard more than I'd ever need to know about two-year-old Isabelle and three-year-old Edward.

The bragging finally ended when Darren parked the car. He'd chosen a small Italian bistro situated several doors down from Needle Me. The moment we stepped inside, I realized he'd most likely made the reservation before he knew of my visit.

Firenza's featured linen tablecloths, soft lighting with candles on each table, and Andrea Bocelli piped through the sound system. A perfect restaurant for an intimate date, not for a couple dragging along a *faux* aunt. I would have apologized for ruining his plans, but even I didn't know before yesterday that I'd be spending the weekend in Oakmont, Pennsylvania.

After we'd given the waitress our orders, I attempted to prolong the conversation about Darren's kids. Anything to keep him talking rather than asking questions. "Given your children's names, is their mother a big *Twilight* fan?"

"You have no idea," he muttered.

"Candace wanted Darren to have his teeth filed into vampire points," said Erica. "Can you imagine?"

"Only one of many reasons why we're now divorced," he said, "but let's get back to you, Anastasia. What types of artworks do you show in your gallery?"

Damn! "Crafts, mainly. Erica mentioned you're a college

admissions counselor at Pitt?"

"That's right. What's the name of the gallery?"

Luckily, I'd anticipated having to supply a gallery name. "Creative Hearts & Hands." The gallery did exist but in Hoboken, not Manhattan. And of course, I wasn't the owner. "How long have you worked at the university?"

Darren frowned as he broke a breadstick in half. "Is this a genetic trait common to all Miller women? You're exactly like Erica. Neither one of you is willing to talk much about yourself. Erica and I have dated for three months, yet I know next to nothing about her life before she moved to Oakmont. She doesn't even have any family photos."

Erica placed her hand on his forearm. "Darren, I told you I lost everything when my house flooded during Hurricane Irene."

He ignored her and turned to me. "What about you, Anastasia? Did your house also flood during the hurricane?"

I hadn't expected the conversation to veer in this direction. Good thing Erica provided a handy dodge for both of us. "Yes, as a matter of fact—"

He slammed his hands on the table, nearly toppling our wine glasses. "Why are you both so damn secretive?"

I shrugged. "I'd love to tell you, Darren, but then I'd have to kill you."

He didn't get the joke. His eyes nearly bugged out of his head. "You're a government agent?"

I laughed. This must be how Zack feels whenever I question him about his frequent spur-of-the-moment trips to remote parts of the world.

Erica placed her hand over Darren's. "Really, does Anastasia look like a government agent? You think she's Jane Bond or something?"

"I can assure you," I said, "that I'm not a spy." At least that wasn't a lie, unlike nearly everything else I'd told Darren so far this evening.

"I'm not sure what to think," he said. "Something's very odd about the way the two of you act. Like you're hiding something."

"Blame our reticence on our upbringing," I said. "In our family talking about yourself was considered poor manners and frowned upon."

I don't think he bought into my explanation, but he gave up peppering me with questions once our dinners arrived.

~*~

"How exhausting!" I said after Darren dropped us off back at Erica's house. "I don't know how you manage hiding your past from everyone. How do you keep all the lies straight?"

Erica curled up on the couch and hugged one of the throw pillows to her chest. "It's a full-time job. I have to think about everything I say before I say anything. On more than one occasion I've slipped and mentioned something I shouldn't have said."

"Like what?"

"A few weeks ago, I told someone at work that I'd met Vittorio Versailles before he was murdered."

"Erica!"

"I know. I caught myself in time and said it was part of a literacy fundraiser I'd attended in New York."

"You need to be more careful."

She sighed. "I'm trying. At least I haven't mentioned anything about my family."

"What about me?"

"My real family, I mean. But you saw how annoyed Darren got

this evening. Eventually, I'm going to have to tell him something."

"You need to discuss this with your WitSec handler."

"I haven't told her about Darren yet."

"She doesn't know you're dating someone?"

"No."

"Darren seems serious, Erica. You need to discuss this with her."

She sighed again. "I know. I promise. As soon as we figure out who's leaving me those notes and gifts. I can only deal with one crisis at a time."

"I think I have a plan."

SIX

"We're going to catch him in the act," I said.

"How? There doesn't seem to be any pattern to when the gifts and cards arrive."

"But you said they're appearing with more frequency lately, twice a day or more."

"That's right."

"So chances are he'll show up again at least once before I leave tomorrow. We're going to be waiting for him the moment he steps onto your property."

I laid out my plan. "We'll set an alarm to wake up before dawn. I'll stake out the front of the house, and you'll stake out the back. At some point he'll show up, and we'll have our answer."

"I hope it's not Eldon," said Erica.

"I haven't noticed anyone else other than Darren taking an interest in you." Other than Eldon and Tilly Braunfelter, we hadn't bumped into anyone who seemed to know Erica. I found that quite odd, especially considering she worked at the library.

"Has any other man asked you out? Have you turned down a date with anyone?"

"No one."

Another thought occurred to me, one I hope she didn't confirm. "You haven't signed up for any online dating sites or visited any chat rooms, have you?"

"Of course not!"

"Then you need to think about what you'll say to Eldon because I'm betting he shows up here sometime tomorrow."

~*~

The alarm woke me at four-thirty the next morning. I peeled my eyelids open to the annoying chirping of waking birds and headed for the bathroom. Erica, already dressed in jeans and a T-shirt, met me in the hall. "I'll start a pot of coffee," she mumbled.

"Don't turn on any lights. If he thinks you're awake, he might not leave anything."

"I hope he's an early riser. I'd love to catch him, then go back to bed."

I yawned. "That makes two of us."

By the dim glow of the bathroom night light, I brushed my teeth and grabbed a quick shower. The sky had begun to lighten when I returned to the guest bedroom. Glancing out the window, I noticed a familiar figure jogging down the street, heading away from the house.

I raced down the stairs, unlocked the front door, and flung it open. No package. No card. Nothing in front of the door, nothing sitting on either porch chair.

"Who is it?" asked Erica, coming up behind me.

"No one." I closed and locked the door. "Is Eldon a runner?"

"I don't know. Why?"

"I saw him jogging down the street."

"But he didn't leave anything on the porch?"

"No. Unless he went to the back door."

"I didn't hear anyone."

We both headed for the kitchen. Erica unlocked and opened the kitchen door. Again, no package or envelope.

"Maybe the jogger only looked like Eldon," I said. After all, I'd met Eldon only once and had spent less than a minute with him.

We both grabbed coffee and cereal bars and took up our stake-out positions. The sun rose; the street came alive. One by one families left to go to church. The morning dragged on without any sign of Eldon or anyone else bearing gifts for Erica.

A little before eleven o'clock Erica called from the kitchen. "I made a fresh pot of coffee."

I grabbed my cup and headed for the kitchen. As Erica poured the coffee, we heard a knock on the front door.

"That's probably Darren," she said.

I followed her to the living room. When she opened the door, we found Horace Buckwalter standing on her porch. He held a bouquet of pink roses in his hands. Mr. Buckwalter offered Erica the flowers. "I've come a'courtin', Rose." Then seeing me, he tipped his hat and said, "With your permission, of course, ma'am."

~*~

Erica invited Mr. Buckwalter into her home and served him a cup of coffee and a plate of cookies. After several phone calls, she tracked down his daughter Ruth.

Fifteen minutes later Ruth arrived to pick up her father. "I'm sorry he disturbed you," she said. "My mother grew up in this house. Her name was Rose Salzwedel. In my father's mind, he must have gone back to his youth when he and my mother first met and dated."

"That explains the gifts and cards," said Erica.

"He brought you gifts?"

"I thought I had a stalker. Someone keeps leaving me cards and presents. Only I didn't know my mystery suitor was your father until this morning." Erica retrieved the box from the pantry and showed her the contents.

Ruth recognized the embroideries at once. "My mother made these."

"That explains all the roses," I said, "and signing the cards with a drawing of a rose."

"But why would your father secretly give me these gifts?" asked Erica.

"Don't you see?" I said. "He thought you were Rose. He was wooing his wife all over again, giving her—you—presents that would mean something to her."

"Oh." Erica looked across the table to where Horace Buckwalter munched on a cookie. He stopped chewing and smiled at her. "You always did bake the best oatmeal raisin cookies, Rose."

No matter that Erica had served him from a bag of Oreos. In Horace's mind, Rose had baked him oatmeal raisin cookies. Erica reached across the table and squeezed Horace's hand. "I'm glad you're enjoying them, Horace."

~*~

I left that evening knowing that for now, at least, Erica was safe. No one had stalked her, and no hit men had arrived in Oakmont to settle a score for her father.

"Remember," I said when she dropped me off at the airport, "you promised me you'd tell your WitSec handler about Darren."

"I will."

I doubted she'd keep her promise.

"We can't have any further contact," I said.

"I know."

I gave her a hug before heading into the terminal. I had a feeling Erica wouldn't keep that promise, either.

MOSAIC MAYHEM

ONE

Not again! I stared down at the barrel of a big black bad-ass gun pointed at my chest. Ever since last winter when Karl Pollack, my not-so-dearly-departed husband, died suddenly, people have been trying to kill me. First, Karl's loan shark. Then a crazy co-worker. Most recently, a hired assassin.

My name is Anastasia Pollack. I'm a debt-ridden, pear-shaped, middle-aged single mom, and crafts editor at a woman's magazine. I'm also apparently a killer magnet, not only in my home state of New Jersey but also across the Atlantic Ocean in Spain.

Worst of all, unlike my three previous run-ins with killers, I had no idea who this guy was or why he wanted me dead. He apparently didn't speak English, and my Spanish is limited to a few words and phrases picked up from watching *Sesame Street* years ago with my kids. My Catalan is non-existent.

So much for a quick getaway to Barcelona.

After the relief of finding that my passport hadn't expired, I thought my biggest problem would be arranging extra care for my semi-invalid mother-in-law during my three-day absence. Silly me.

I landed in this situation thanks to Zack. When Karl dropped dead, leaving me with debt that rivaled the gross national product of an average third-world country, I was forced to rent out the apartment over my garage and move my studio to my dingy, unheated basement. Little did I know at the time that my new tenant, award-winning photojournalist and possible spy (although he vehemently denies the latter) Zachary Barnes, would segue from renter to lover.

Zack looks like his DNA cavorted in the gene pools of George Clooney, Pierce Brosnan, Patrick Dempsey, and Antonio Bandares. What he sees in me, I'll never know, and yet here we are—a couple. I'm not complaining.

I'd spent most of the summer working a second job every weekend, and I was beyond exhausted. So when Zack invited me to tag along with him while he photographed architect Antoni Gaudi's Parc Güell for a *National Geographic* spread, I cashed in some of my comp time and packed a bag.

We arrived in Barcelona early in the morning, dropped our luggage at a hotel off Plaça de Catalunya, and headed to the park, a fairytale inspired masterpiece that resembled a miniature city. While Zack took a meeting with the director in Torre Rosa, the park's museum and former Gaudi home, I wandered the enchanting grounds and buildings, snapping photos of the whimsical Hansel and Gretel gatehouses, the Sala Hipostila marketplace with its multi-domed ceiling, and the main terrace, ringed with an intricately decorated serpentine bench—all embellished with Gaudi's trademark mosaics. I planned to use the photos as part of a feature on mosaic art for a future issue of *American Woman*, the magazine where I worked.

Afterwards, I set off on one of the many trails weaving through nearly forty acres of steep hillside in order to enjoy some of the spectacular views of the city spread out below. I was in a secluded area with no one else around when a bear of a man with a short dark beard that did little to hide his acne scarred cheeks stepped from the wooded area onto the path in front of me. Like so many other men on the streets of Barcelona, he wore a red and gold soccer jersey, but unlike all the others, this guy accessorized his outfit with a deadly weapon.

A gasp froze in my throat.

He might as well have been speaking Swahili for all the good my *Sesame Street* Spanish did me. Zack had warned me that pickpockets trolled the streets of Barcelona, preying on hapless tourists. He hadn't mentioned anything about armed gunmen, but common sense told me I was being robbed.

"Take it," I said, dropping my handbag at his feet. But this was no robbery. He didn't scoop up my bag and run. Instead, he grabbed both the bag and my arm.

With the gun jabbing me in the ribs, he wrapped his other arm tightly around my shoulders and forced me back down the path and across the courtyard filled with oblivious tourists who ignored me as I tried to make eye contact and silently mouthed, "Help me."

As he led me through the main gates onto the street, several self-defense options came to mind—stomping my heel into his instep, twisting my body to knee him in the groin, screaming at the top of my lungs. Preferably all three at once. The gun barrel poking my midsection forced me to discount all of them, even after he marched me down a deserted alley, zip-tied my hands behind my back, placed a sack over my head, and shoved me into the back of a mud-spattered black panel truck.

Better alive and kidnapped than bleeding out on the street, I figured. But why me? I had no money, no political connections that might figure into the Catalan separatist movement. Had he wanted to rape or murder me, he could have pulled me into the woods back at the park. No one would have seen or heard anything. I don't know whether it was intuition or past experience, but something told me I didn't need to fear for my life.

After a bruise-inducing ride around sharp turns, the truck finally came to a stop a few minutes later. My abductor hauled me out and dragged me up a flight of steps into a building. When he yanked the sack off my head, I found myself standing in front of an ornately carved massive desk in a room reminiscent of a nineteenth century American robber baron's library. Floor-to-ceiling stained glass windows filled the one wall not covered in floor-to-ceiling bookcases.

Behind the desk sat a man with a full head of silver hair and a matching goatee. Dressed in a charcoal gray three-piece pinstripe suit, he exuded a cultured, sophisticated air that reminded me of certain James Bond villains—until he smiled, showing off a mouthful of nicotine-stained teeth. "Welcome, Señora."

"Who are you, and what do you want?"

"Who I am is not important. What I want is the ransom your husband will pay to get you back unharmed."

"You obviously have me confused with someone else. I don't have a husband."

He made a tsking sound with his tongue and shook his head in a gesture of disappointment. "There's no sense in lying to me,

Señora Naiman. I know very well who you are. And I know your husband will pay handsomely to have you returned safely."

"Would that be the no-good deadbeat who died last winter? Because that's the only husband I've ever had, and his name wasn't Naiman."

Anger settled over his face. "Enough games!" He slammed his hand on the desk. "We will call your husband."

"Good luck with that. Unless, of course, you have a direct line to hell."

He reached for his phone, punched in a number, and pushed the speaker phone button.

"Hello?"

In a calm, controlled voice my captor said, "Señor Naiman, listen carefully. I am holding your wife. You will deposit one hundred million Euros into the Swiss bank account I'm texting to your phone to secure her safe return."

"I don't know who you are or what kind of scam you're running, bub, but my wife is standing right beside me." He then disconnected the call.

"Your husband has little regard for your welfare," he said to me. "That is troubling. For you, especially."

"That wasn't my husband."

"Señora Naiman, Elaine—"

"My name is not Elaine Naiman!"

He snapped his fingers and pointed to the bag my kidnapper still held.

When his goon deposited my handbag on the desk, he upended it to retrieve my passport. His mouth tightened and his eyes narrowed as he stared at the information. He slammed the passport onto his desk and launched into a rapid-fire Spanish tirade directed at the goon.

Goon Guy whipped out his phone, pointed to the screen, then pointed to me while he argued his case. His boss wasn't buying it. He grabbed the phone and hurled it across the room, shattering a large porcelain urn—Renaissance era if I remembered my art history lessons. I cringed at the senseless destruction of such a valuable artifact. Then he pointed to the door and screamed something that I didn't need translated. Goon Guy beat a hasty retreat.

My silver-haired captor placed the items spilled across his desk back into my handbag. "I am sorry for the misunderstanding, Señora Pollack. Juan will bring you back to Parc Güell."

He rounded his desk and tucked my bag between my torso and my still bound arm, then exited the room. Juan the Goon reentered, placed the sack back over my head, and dragged me out the building, down the steps, and back into the van.

A few minutes later I once again walked through the entryway of Parc Güell, the red welts on my wrists the only evidence of my short but harrowing ordeal. I've lived through far worse. I parked myself outside the entrance of Torre Rosa and waited for Zack to finish his meeting.

In my experience, most guys are less than observant, but Zack zeroed in on my sore wrists the moment he stepped from the building. I should have kept my hands behind my back.

"What happened?" he asked.

Before I'd uttered more than two sentences, he whisked me into the museum office, quickly explained the situation to the director, then placed a call to the police. While we awaited their arrival, the director accessed an article from the *London Times*. "Take a look at this," he said, pointing to a photo on his computer screen. "Definitely a striking resemblance."

With a few major exceptions. Elaine Naiman looked like I might look if I could afford a live-in trainer, daily spa treatments, and the occasional nip/tuck. I could be her frumpy cousin—maybe—definitely not her twin. Anyone who mistook me for her needed an eye exam.

I scanned the article which detailed a charity auction held a week earlier. Mr. and Mrs. Michael Naiman had donated a Brancusi to an auction to raise funds for the removal of landmines in Somalia.

"If they have that kind of money, it certainly explains why someone is trying to kidnap her for ransom. Who are these people?"

"Michael Naiman owns Global Armament," said Zack.

Why was I not surprised he knew of the man? "Is that as frightening as it sounds?"

"GA manufactures missiles and bombs."

"Holy irony."

"More so than you realize," said the museum director. He turned to Zack. "That opening I invited you to this evening at the Museu Picasso?"

"What about it?"

"The paintings are from the Naimans' private collection."

"How much money does this guy have?" I asked.

"Rumors estimate his net worth as greater than that of Trump, Soros, and Buffet combined," said Zack. "But they're only rumors. No one knows for sure because the company isn't publicly traded."

"How come I've never heard of him?"

"People who make their money dealing in the tools of warfare usually keep a low profile."

I rubbed my sore wrists. "Apparently, not low enough."

When the police arrived, they confirmed that Mr. Naiman had received a phone call from a would-be kidnapper. With Zack acting as translator—who knew he spoke fluent Catalan?—the police asked if I'd be able to pick out my kidnappers from mug shots.

"Definitely."

After the police escorted us to the station, I spent the next half hour flipping through mug shots until I found both men. As a trained artist, I'm used to noticing details. Each man had enough distinct facial features that I had no trouble identifying them. Juan Balaguer, AKA Goon Guy and Esteve Laporta AKA the older guy with the silver hair, goatee, and brown teeth.

"These men are part of a local crime syndicate run by Carlos Perella," said another officer who joined us. He introduced himself as Captain De la Riva. Tall and thin with a high forehead, receding hairline, and a jet-black pencil-thin mustache, he spoke in flawless English. "Balaguer is a low-level enforcer; Laporta is higher up the organization's chain of command. Señor Perella has never gotten involved in kidnapping for profit before—at least not that we know of—he's mostly into smuggling and money laundering, but I suppose there's a first time for everything."

"What happens now?" I asked.

"That's up to you, Señora Pollack. We can pick up Balaguer and Laporta and charge them with kidnapping, but you'd have to be available to testify in court."

"We're only here for two more days."

"Even so," De La Riva continued, "given Perella's resources, the charges probably wouldn't stick. He's like your Teflon Don back in the States."

"Hardly. John Gotti died in prison. Perella is very much alive and walking free."

"We can offer you police protection while you're here."

"I don't think that's necessary. They won't make the same mistake twice. But what about Elaine Naiman? She's their real target."

"Her husband declined our offer. He has his own private security force to protect them both."

"Then our business here is done," I said.

"That blew a sizable chunk of our first day in Barcelona," I said as Zack and I left the police station.

He squeezed my hand. "It could have been a lot worse."

"I know." An involuntary shudder ran through me at the thought of the gruesome alternatives. I'd been damn lucky.

TWO

Since Zack's real work began tomorrow when Parc Güell would open two hours late in order to give him time to photograph the premises without tourists getting in the way of his shots, we had the rest of the day to ourselves. After a lunch of tapas and sangria, he took me on a whirlwind tour of Barcelona that included Gaudi's masterpiece, La Sagrada Família, a one-hundred-thirty-year-old, still-under construction basilica that looked like Gaudi had created it by dripping wet sand.

At any other time, I would have marveled at the art and architecture, but I found myself too distracted, filled with a sense that someone was following me. I held tight to Zack's hand and continually darted glances over my shoulder. He kept up a lively banter, trying to put me at ease. Although he didn't succeed, I forced myself to take part in the conversation.

"Makes you wonder if he worked under the influence of hallucinogens," I said, half an hour later as I stared up at the mosaic embellished wavy facade of Casa Batlló, a building, like so much of Gaudi's other work, completely devoid of straight lines. I'd never seen such fantastical architecture outside of DisneyWorld.

"He certainly wouldn't be the first artist to do so," said Zack.

"A painting created under the influence is one thing, but buildings that have stood for over a hundred years?" I shook my head, stealing another glance around the street as I did so. "Doubtful."

~*~

The Museu Picasso, a series of five adjacent Gothic-baroque mansions, showcased the artist's pre-cubist work. The Naiman collection filled three connecting rooms off an inner courtyard. Under normal circumstances, I would have been excited to attend the opening of a museum exhibit. However, tonight I was far more interested in the two guests of honor than any of the Picassos. I figured Elaine Naiman would be easy to spot. I simply had to look for a better-looking, better-dressed version of me.

I spied her the moment we entered the gallery. She wore a ruby red strapless taffeta cocktail dress that skimmed the top of her knees. A thick diamond choker wrapped around her long Audrey Hepburn neck, catching the lights and sparkling from across the room. Additional diamonds dripped from her earlobes, adorned her upswept hairdo, and clad both her wrists and multiple fingers. Most hip-hop tycoons wore less bling. Any one of Elaine's baubles would pay off my entire Karl-induced debt and then some.

She and her husband held court in the center of the main room displaying their collection. Michael Naiman, a balding middle-aged man carrying too much weight for his less-than-average height, kept a chubby arm wrapped firmly around his wife's waspish waist as they spoke with other guests. Men in black stood off to the side, continually scanning the room.

As Zack and I inched our way toward them, Elaine and I made eye contact. She wriggled out from her husband's grasp and headed in our direction, surprise filling her face. Two of the security detail followed her. "We must be related," she said, scanning me from head to toe. She held out her hand. "Elaine Naiman."

"Anastasia Pollack," I said, shaking her hand. "And this is Zachary Barnes."

Elaine nodded at Zack. "Mr. Barnes."

Zack returned the gesture. "Mrs. Naiman."

"I don't know if we're related," I said, "but we definitely have something in common."

"And what is that?"

"I'm the person who was kidnapped earlier today by someone who mistook me for you."

Elaine's eyes grew wide as she gasped. Her hand flew to her décolletage. "Kidnapped? Are you kidding?"

"You don't know?"

"No one said a word to me about any kidnapping. I hope you weren't harmed."

Odd since her husband claimed she was standing right beside him when Laporta called. "No, they let me go when they realized they had the wrong person."

"Where did this happen?"

"At Parc Güell this morning."

"I went to Parc Güell this morning."

Naiman chose that moment to join us. Elaine turned to him. "Do you know anything about someone trying to kidnap me today?"

"It was a hoax," he said, placing his arm back around her waist.

"Someone trying to extort money. I saw no reason to worry you."

"It was no hoax," I said.

Naiman raised both eyebrows. "And how would you know that?"

I stole a quick glance at Zack and could tell his wheels spun as quickly as mine. Someone was lying, and my money was on the guy who built bombs for a living.

"Because the kidnappers grabbed me, thinking I was your wife."

Naiman's dismissive head-to-toe once-over of me silently stated he didn't believe anyone could mistake me for his wife. On that much, I had to agree.

"How do I know you weren't in on it?" he asked.

"That's ridiculous. If I were, would I be stupid enough to show up here and speak with your wife?"

"Most criminals are stupid," he said. "That's why they eventually get caught."

I glared at him. He glared back. Then he dismissed me by turning his back and dragging his wife toward another group of guests.

"Something doesn't add up," I said.

"No, it doesn't," said Zack, "but it's not our problem. Let's grab some wine and look at the paintings."

We were sipping sangria in front of *L'Ascète*, the portrait of an elderly man painted during Picasso's Blue Period, when Elaine Naiman joined us. "My husband's most prized possession," she said with a nod to the painting and a scowl on her face. "He claims the model is his great-grandfather, the founder of Global Armament."

"Is it?" I asked, surprised she'd come back to speak with us but not surprised to find two of the men in black shadowing her. A quick scan of the room showed Michael Naiman being interviewed by a television crew off in one corner of the room. He might keep a low profile back in the states, but he certainly courted the press in Europe.

Elaine laughed. "Highly unlikely." Then she sobered and placed her hand on my arm. "I want to apologize for the way Michael treated you."

"He should be the one apologizing," said Zack.

She sighed. "That's not going to happen." Then she turned to me. "Let me make it up to you. Have brunch with me tomorrow. I'm convinced we must be related, and I'd like to figure out how. Where are you staying?"

"The Regina."

"Shall I send a car for you at nine?"

Since Zack would be tied up for several hours the next morning, I agreed. Elaine glanced over her shoulder. The interview showed no signs of ending. "Looks like I have time to powder my nose," she said. "See you tomorrow."

She headed in the direction of the ladies' room. Zack and I moved on to the next painting. A moment later the museum plunged into darkness, and shots rang out. A woman screamed.

Thick smoke filled the room. Panic ensued.

"Tear gas," said Zack. "Try not to breathe." I clamped one hand over my mouth and nose. My eyes and lungs burned.

All around us people stampeded, plowing into each other as we all desperately sought an exit. Whoever had pulled the plug also disabled the emergency lights. Zack held fast to my arm and dragged me along in the pitch blackness to what I hoped would be fresh air.

We finally made it to the museum courtyard and collapsed against a stone wall. The courtyard filled with the sounds of coughing, gagging, and retching as others joined us, their bodies barely visible from the only available light, a half-moon darting in and out of the clouds. In the distance I heard approaching sirens.

Several minutes later the symptoms of the tear gas began to abate. Murmurs of speculation about what had happened replaced the coughing, gagging, and retching. Everyone suspected an art heist, but no one was willing to reenter the gallery to confirm that hypothesis.

After a few minutes the lights came back on. The police streamed into the courtyard and herded us all into a room in one of the other museum buildings. Several people had sustained injuries during the stampede. A few showed signs of concussion while at least one woman had suffered a broken wrist when she tripped and fell.

While medics treated the injured, an officer made his way around the room, checking our names against the official guest list. Detectives began questioning everyone. As I waited, I scanned the room. "I don't see the Naimans or their bodyguards."

"Not everyone from the opening is here," said Zack. "Some people probably took refuge elsewhere in the museum and are being questioned in another area."

That made sense. Except a minute later Michael Naiman stormed into the room, his men in black following close on his heels. "Elaine!" he yelled. He stopped at the entrance, scoping out the clusters of people while his men branched out around the room.

Not finding Elaine among us, Naiman turned to one of the detectives and demanded, "Where the hell is my wife?"

THREE

Elaine Naiman had disappeared.

"I saw her heading in the direction of the ladies' room just as the lights went out," I told the detective standing nearest to me.

Naiman heard me and pounced. "You again!" He marched across the room and pointed a stubby finger at me. "You're involved in this somehow. What have you done with my wife?" He tried to grab my arm, but Zack stepped between us and blocked him.

Naiman turned to the detective. "I want them arrested."

"On what charges?" The three of us spun around. Captain De la Riva, flanked by two officers, stood at the entrance to the room.

"I don't care what you charge them with." Naiman turned back to me and Zack. "My men will get to the bottom of this, and when they do, you'll spend the rest of your lives in a Barcelona jail."

One thing I've learned from my recent interactions with the police back home is that they don't take kindly to civilians poking around on their turf. Captain De la Riva was no different. He bristled. "Mr. Naiman, you and your men will leave this investigation to me and my department, or you'll find yourself charged with obstruction."

Michael Naiman was a man used to giving orders, not taking them. He bristled back. "Then do your job. Find my wife. And do it fast, or I'll have your badge."

So not the right thing to say to the man. A moment later two officers escorted a handcuffed Michael Naiman from the room.

~*~

My harrowing experience earlier in the day, coupled with my presence at the museum, also seemed too coincidental for Captain De la Riva. He requested I return to the station for additional questioning. At least no one handcuffed me before escorting me from the building.

Once at the police station, Zack and I were led into De la Riva's office rather than into separate interrogation rooms. I took that to mean he—hopefully—didn't believe Naiman's accusations against me. The captain motioned to the two straight-backed wooden chairs on one side of his cluttered desk as he settled into a more comfortable chair behind the desk.

"What can you tell me about the events at the museum?" he asked.

Zack and I informed him of our two conversations with Elaine Naiman. "Someone lied," I said. "When Laporta called him, I heard Naiman claim Elaine was in the room with him, but Elaine told us she knew nothing about the call or an attempted abduction.

"She also said she was at Parc Güell this morning," added Zack.

"Why were the two of you at the museum this evening?" asked De la Riva.

"We were invited by the director of Parc Güell," said Zack. "You can check with him."

"I will. Meanwhile, I'm going to have to request you hand over your passports."

"Why?" I asked.

"Because we can't have you leaving the country during this investigation. You're a crucial witness and possibly even—how do you say it in America? A person of interest."

"But I have to get home to my children."

"You'd better make other arrangements for them."

"For how long?"

"For as long as it takes to find Elaine Naiman."

I jumped to my feet, nearly toppling my chair, and leaned halfway across the desk separating us. My entire body shook. I don't know which was greater, my fear or my rage. "I had nothing to do with her disappearance. I'll prove it. Give me a lie detector test."

"Sit down, Mrs. Pollack!"

Zack placed his hand on my arm and guided me back into the chair. Tears filled my eyes. What if this case turned into an Amanda Knox type fiasco? I could wind up unjustly confined to a Barcelona prison for years. My kids might have kids of their own before I won my release.

De la Riva leaned back in his chair, steepled his fingers under his chin, and segued into a more fatherly attitude, one he probably learned in Interrogations 101 back at the police academy. "For what it's worth, Mrs. Pollack, I believe you, but I still cannot have you leave the country until I get to the bottom of this."

I needed him to consider other possible suspects with likely motives, scenarios that didn't involve me.

Think, Anastasia!

I had taken an instant dislike to Michael Naiman. His condescending attitude toward me, not to mention his accusations, reminded me of every super-smug, ego-driven misogynist with whom I'd ever crossed paths. And I'd crossed paths with quite a few over my forty-two years. Powerful, wealthy individuals like Michael Naiman did what they wanted when they wanted, trampling anyone who dared to cross them.

Then it hit me. Maybe that's exactly what was going on here. I fought back the tears, took a deep breath, and tossed out the most logical of theories based on watching and reading decades of national news headlines. "I'll bet Naiman is behind his wife's disappearance."

O.J. Simpson, Scott Peterson, Drew Peterson, Charles Stuart—more often than not, and despite how much they present themselves as grieving husbands, back in the States, the perpetrator usually turns out to be the spouse. Why should it be any different in Barcelona?

"What are you suggesting?" asked De la Riva.

"Were any paintings stolen?"

"None."

No surprise there. Tonight's attack had nothing to do with an art heist and everything to do with an heiress heist. "Maybe Naiman orchestrated both incidents to get rid of his wife permanently—setting the stage with a bogus kidnapping attempt earlier in the day prior to tonight's actual abduction."

"To create plausible deniability?"

"Exactly." The more I thought about it, the more sense it made—especially since everything about Michael Naiman sent the needle on my Creepometer soaring well past the red zone.

"Think about it. He doesn't tell his wife about the first attempt, then brushes it off as a hoax when she learns of it and confronts him. Yet he alerted you about the ransom demand."

"But you told us Balaguer and Laporta didn't realize they'd grabbed the wrong woman. If they were working for Naiman—"

"Why assume they were working for Naiman?" asked Zack. "Someone else would have orchestrated everything, keeping Naiman's hands far from any taint. They set up Perella's organization to misdirect your investigation. Anastasia identifies her kidnappers as two of Perella's henchmen, and the police go after the syndicate for an attempted kidnapping. No one suspects Naiman. When Elaine is actually abducted, you've got a prior attempt—one that Naiman reported to you—already on record. And the kidnappers already fingered."

"Don't forget," I added, "Naiman refused police protection for his wife."

"That's true," said De la Riva.

"Did you ever speak directly with Elaine Naiman after you interviewed me earlier today?" I asked.

He shook his head. "Her husband didn't want to worry her."

"Of course he didn't. And now we know why. Let's not worry the little lady. Wealthy hubby will handle everything for her." Typical male chauvinism coupled with music to the ears of a cash-strapped police department. De la Riva's budget wouldn't take a hit to supply protection to a tourist.

I pressed on with my theory. "I'll bet he's got a mistress waiting in the wings to become the next Mrs. Michael Naiman. For a man of his means, murder would be a much cheaper solution than divorce. What's one more dead body to him? He deals in death on a daily basis."

De la Riva stroked his chin. "An interesting theory, Mrs. Pollack. One worth pursuing further." He held out his hand. "But I still need your passports."

We had no choice. Zack and I reluctantly turned over our documents.

As we headed back to the hotel, I asked, "What am I going to do? I can't stay here indefinitely. I need to get home."

Zack wrapped his arm around my shoulders and drew me close. "We'll figure something out. I'll contact the U.S. consulate tomorrow to see if they can pull a few strings."

Would the consulate pull strings for a photojournalist and his girlfriend inadvertently caught up in a kidnapping investigation? Ever since we met, I've worried Zack might really work for one of the alphabet agencies. For the first time I hoped he did.

~*~

Zack and I ate an early breakfast the next morning before he left for Parc Güell. "Are you sure you're okay with being alone for a few hours?" he asked.

Part of me wanted to tag along with him, but another part of me had no desire to return to the place where this ongoing nightmare started. "Sure. The kidnappers have who they want. They let me go even though I saw their faces. I don't think I have to worry."

"All the same, maybe you should hang around the hotel until I return. I'll only be a few hours."

"Maybe I'll just go back to bed." Neither of us had slept much after returning to the hotel the previous night. This relaxing three-day getaway had turned into anything but.

"Good idea. Keep the bed warm for me." He slung his camera bag over his shoulder, kissed me good-bye, and headed out.

I lingered over another cup of coffee while catching up on some pleasure reading, an activity I rarely had time for at home. I'd just finished the third chapter of Emma Carlyle's *Four Uncles and a Wedding*, when the last person on earth I expected to see that morning approached my table.

"I need your help," said Michael Naiman, his left hand firmly gripped around the handles of a large black leather artist's portfolio. He hadn't shaved, and he still wore the tuxedo from the previous night. However, the two men in black standing with arms crossed several paces behind him countered any sympathy his classic grieving husband persona attempted to solicit from me.

I stared at him for a full ten seconds, biting my tongue the entire time, before I spoke. "Last night you accused me of involvement in your wife's abduction, and this morning you want my help?"

"I have no other choice."

"Well, I do, and the answer is no."

"You can't—"

"I can't what? Say no to you? Guess again. I'm not one of your black-suited flunkies. I don't take orders from you."

"I'm not—"

"Before yesterday I'd never heard of you. Yet in less than twenty-four hours I'm first kidnapped in place of your wife, then accused of being an accessory to the crime. I have children back in the States. A job. A life. Now, thanks to you, I'm stuck in Barcelona until the police find out what really happened."

I speared him with the most disdainful glare I could muster after a night of little sleep. "You're the last person I'd go out of my way to help." Then I turned my attention back to my book, dismissing him in much the same manner he'd dismissed me the night before.

Naiman didn't take the hint and leave. Instead, like the overbearing egomaniac he was, he slammed his pudgy hand over the page. "Even if helping me gets you home on time?"

I looked up to see desperation written across his face. Either he possessed exemplary acting skills, or my theory of his involvement in Elaine's disappearance was totally off-base. On the slim chance he spoke the truth, I decided to listen. "You have thirty seconds."

He pulled out the chair opposite me and sat. Before speaking, he raised his arm, snapped his fingers, and pointed to the espresso machine. One of his flunkies headed over to the breakfast buffet to prepare a cup for him. Talk about the height of hubris! "Your time is ticking away," I said.

He continued to sit silently staring at me while waiting for his coffee. When it arrived, he took a sip before speaking. "I'll admit, I didn't believe you at first, and I'm still not sure I do. I had my men look into your background. I know you're up to your eyeballs in debt."

"This is how you try to convince me to help you? You're not doing yourself any good, and your childish power play used up your time." I stood to leave.

"Or maybe you were merely a victim of unfortunate circumstances, in the wrong place at the wrong time."

I folded my arms across my chest and looked down my nose at him. "*Maybe?*"

He exhaled his frustration. "All right. I'll give you the benefit of the doubt."

"How *noblesse oblige* of you."

"Please." He indicated my empty chair. "Hear me out."

"Why should I?"

"Because I'm begging you."

He said the words as if it killed him to utter them. Men like Michael Naiman don't beg. They demand. I lowered myself into the chair.

"I received another phone call from the same man who originally claimed to have Elaine."

"Go on."

"He's got her this time."

"I still don't see how this involves me. Tell the police. I identified the men who took me. They know who they are."

"I can't. They threatened to kill Elaine."

"Then pay the ransom. From what I hear, a hundred million Euros barely makes a dent in your bank account."

He scrubbed his hand over his stubbled jaw line. "I've already transferred the money, but now he's demanding something else. One of my paintings."

I pointed to the portfolio. "Are you on your way to make the exchange?"

"The kidnapper is demanding you bring him the painting."

"*Me?* Why me?"

"I don't know, but now you see why I still have my suspicions about you."

I suppose if I were in his position, I'd have suspicions about me, as well. "If I give him the painting, he releases Elaine?"

"That's the deal. But no one else can know. Not the police. Not your boyfriend. No one."

"I don't know where to find him. The guy who nabbed me put a sack over my head and threw me in the back of a panel truck."

"He said he'd find you."

"Like you did? How did you know where I'm staying?"

"I have certain resources at my disposal."

"I'll bet you do."

"Will you deliver the painting?"

Did I have any choice? Once Elaine was freed, Zack and I would be able to catch our scheduled flight home. "For Elaine, not you."

He nodded, then stood. I suppose a thank-you was too much to expect. He'd used up his annual allotment of humility when he'd begged for my help.

"Which painting?" I asked as he turned and took a few steps in the direction of the exit.

He returned to the table. "*L'Ascète.* I had to retrieve it from the museum without the police finding out."

His most prized possession, according to his wife. Interesting. If Michael Naiman was willing to part with something he valued more than any of his other possessions, maybe he really did love his wife and want her back. "You stole your own painting?"

"It's not stealing; I own it. The painting was only on loan to the museum."

I grabbed hold of the portfolio handles and stared at his departing back as he strode across the near-empty hotel breakfast room. The painting was worth millions.

Now what? Was I supposed to stay in the hotel until someone contacted me or stroll around Plaça de Catalunya, awaiting the arrival of a muddy black panel truck? What if someone yanked the portfolio out of my hand before I made the exchange?

Staying in the hotel seemed the best option. With my hand clenched so firmly around the portfolio handles that my knuckles turned white, I headed for the elevator. The doors opened. I stepped inside and pushed the button for the third floor. The next thing I knew, a man wearing mirrored sunglasses and a Panama hat pulled low over his face stuck an umbrella between the doors to prevent them from closing. The doors sprang back open, and he stepped inside.

FOUR

I kept my head down and inched away from him.

"Do not be afraid, Señora Pollack."

I recognized his voice. I stole a glance upward. He smiled. Brown teeth. Laporta. "Have you come for the painting?"

"Sí," He wrapped his hand around my arm. "But first we will go to your room."

I gasped and tried to pull away from him.

He held fast. "I will not harm you."

"Why do you need to go to my room?" I shoved the portfolio at him. "Here's the painting. Take it."

"I must examine it first."

I suppose that made sense, but I still wasn't crazy about letting him into my room. I weighed my options as the elevator ascended. Laporta was probably pushing seventy. As long as he didn't pull a knife or gun on me, I could probably defend myself, assuming he didn't know any martial arts. But how likely was it that a member of a crime syndicate traveled without a weapon on him?

The elevator arrived on the third floor, and the doors opened. Laporta knew which way to turn and escorted me down the hall, stopping in front of the door to my room. I didn't bother asking how he knew which room was mine. He'd probably paid off the desk clerk.

When he pulled a key card from his pocket, my suspicions were confirmed. After unlocking the door, he waved me inside. He grabbed the *Do Not Disturb* sign from the interior door handle, placed it on the outer handle, then closed and locked the door. My breakfast threatened to regurgitate.

Laporta was all business, though. He took the portfolio from me and removed *L'Ascète*. The nearly three feet by four feet painting had been removed from its frame but was still mounted on stretcher bars.

He placed the painting on the bed and removed a folding knife from his pants pocket. I stepped back, flattening myself against the dresser, but he paid no attention to me. He opened the knife and carefully slid the blade between the back of the painting and the stretcher bars. Taking his time, he slowly drew the blade back and forth along the wood.

He'd made his way three-quarters around the painting when he stopped. He withdrew the blade, bringing with it a sliver thin microchip.

Laporta pocketed the chip, then placed the painting back in the portfolio. He held out his hand, "Your phone, *por favor*, Señora."

I removed my phone from my purse and handed it to him. He turned it off and dropped it back into my purse. "Come," he said. "We will deliver the painting to its new owner." He reached for my arm and together we left the hotel.

As we made our way toward Plaça de Catalunya, Laporta reached into his pocket and withdrew the chip. Half a block later we passed a garbage truck. He flicked his wrist, and the chip sailed into a huge pile of trash.

"Was that a GPS?" I asked.

"Of course. Did you think Naiman wouldn't try to track you and his beloved painting?"

Would Naiman fall for the ruse and think his *L'Ascète* had been destroyed? "You won't be able to sell it."

Laporta chuckled. "You are very naïve, Mrs. Pollack. The world is full of men willing to pay enormous sums to add to their very private collections. But who said anything about selling *L'Ascète*?"

Was this less about the painting and more about a power play between two alpha males? I wondered if Perella and Naiman had history between them. Both dealt in death and destruction in their own ways. Had their paths crossed at one time? How do you get even with a man who has more money than God? You take from him those things that money can't replace—his wife and his painting.

"You will release Elaine Naiman, right?"

He didn't answer me.

We cut across Plaça de Catalunya, then continued down La Rambla, a broad pedestrian thoroughfare, at a leisurely pace. To anyone passing by we appeared to be a father and daughter out for a morning stroll.

"Are you enjoying our glorious city?" he asked after several minutes of silence.

"Oh, yes, being kidnapped and tear gassed were definite high points of my visit."

"For that I am truly sorry."

"I'll bet."

"I hope those unfortunate experiences haven't soured you to Barcelona."

"Why ever would you think that?"

He laughed. "You do have a unique sense of humor, Señora Pollack. I would have enjoyed getting to know you better."

Did that mean he was going to let me go soon or that my days were numbered? "I have children," I said.

"Sí, I know."

What else did he know about me?

We walked for a few more minutes, then he steered me down a narrow alley with shops and apartments on either side. Halfway down the alley we stopped alongside a silver Mercedes. Laporta beeped the locks and opened the trunk.

"Please, no," I inched away from him, but instead of reaching for me, he deposited the portfolio inside the trunk, then slammed the lid shut.

Laporta walked around to the passenger side of the car and opened the door. "Come. We will now go to Mrs. Naiman."

I slid onto the black leather seat and fastened my seatbelt, grateful for the comfort of traveling upright and minus a sack over my head or zip ties binding my wrists.

Laporta drove a circuitous route around the city, often winding back to roads we'd already traversed. Eventually, he took us to the outskirts of town and up into the hills. We drove for over an hour before he pulled down a long winding road flanked by date palms.

I glanced at the dashboard clock. By now Zack would have returned from Parc Güell and found me missing. He wouldn't know about my visit from Michael Naiman. He wouldn't know that Laporta had taken me outside the city. Being geographically challenged, I had no clue if we were even still in Spain. We may have crossed over into France by now. With my phone turned off, Zack wouldn't be able to reach me. No one would know my whereabouts. And that's probably exactly the way Laporta had planned it.

We continued on for about a mile before we came to an iron gate that blocked the remainder of the road. Laporta pressed a series of buttons on a keypad attached to his dashboard. The gates swung open. After he pulled forward, the gates automatically closed behind us.

We drove another mile before arriving at the entrance to an enormous pink Mediterranean villa. I assumed the home belonged to Carlos Perella.

Laporta parked the Mercedes under the massive porte-cochère, retrieved the portfolio from the trunk, then took my arm and escorted me into the villa to a pink marble-tiled foyer larger than my entire house. A white marble fountain adorned with water-spouting cherubs stood in the center of the foyer with a double-winding pink marble staircase branching out from either side. Columned archways leading to other rooms stood to the left and right of the foyer.

Laporta led me through the archway on the left, then down a hallway that opened up into an enormous garden courtyard enclosed on all four sides by the house. Elaine Naiman sat at a glass-topped wrought iron patio table at the far end of the courtyard.

FIVE

Elaine rose as we approached. For someone who had been abducted only hours earlier, she looked amazingly serene with fresh make-up on her face and not a hair out of place on her perfectly coifed head. Rather than the red cocktail dress from the evening before, this morning she wore a pair of white linen trousers, a black silk shell, and an unstructured turquoise linen jacket with deep kangaroo pockets. A single emerald cut diamond hung from a delicate gold chain around her neck. A pair of matching diamond studs graced her earlobes. A vintage diamond bracelet watch completed her accessories. Quite an understated contrast to last night's bling bonanza.

Had her kidnappers allowed her to return home to pack a suitcase before whisking her off into the hills?

"I'm so glad you could join me for brunch this morning," she said, taking both of my hands in hers.

"Brunch?"

"Did you forget? I did say I'd send a car for you at nine o'clock.

And here you are." She poured two glasses of white sangria from a pitcher on the table and handed me one.

"Yes, but under the circumstances—"

She laughed. "You figured brunch was canceled?"

"The thought had crossed my mind."

She waved her hand in the air as if she were swatting away a pesky fly. "Nonsense. I'm looking forward to spending time with you."

She turned to Laporta. "Is that the painting?"

"Sí, Señora." He handed the portfolio to Elaine. "And you were correct in assuming Señor Naiman would attach a tracking device."

"You took care of it?"

"Sí."

"Gracias, Señor Laporta. Please tell Carmesina we're ready for brunch."

"Sí, Señora." Laporta turned and headed toward a set of French doors off to our right.

What the hell was going on here? Elaine certainly didn't act like a kidnapping victim, nor did she sound as though she suffered from Stockholm Syndrome.

"Sit, Anastasia." She waved to one of the two floral cushioned chairs on either side of the table. I settled into one, and she took the other. Then she unzipped the portfolio and withdrew the painting.

"Ah, *L'Ascète*, which of us will he miss more?" She turned to me and smiled. Her eyes twinkled with a combination of mischief and malice. "I'm guessing the damn painting. Wives are too easily replaced, right?"

Everything finally made sense. "You orchestrated everything, didn't you?"

She laughed.

"Why?"

Before she could answer, a servant rolled out a cart filled with place settings and covered dishes. She placed silverware and water glasses on the table in front of us and spread napkins on our laps. Then she poured coffee and served us each a platter containing a frittata with a fruit salad on the side.

"Gracias, Carmesina."

I waited while Elaine took a few bites of her frittata and a sip of coffee before she finally answered my question. Her voice grew hard and tight. "Because Michael Naiman is an abusive monster." Her right hand absently traveled to her throat. That's when I noticed the finger-sized bruises, fading but still visible, on either side of her neck. The diamond choker she'd worn last night had concealed them.

"Why not divorce him?"

Elaine sighed. "There's no way he'd ever let me leave him. Trust me. I've tried. The man is ruthless. This was my only option. I now have a hundred million Euros which will enable me to disappear. A bit of plastic surgery, a new identity, and Michael will never find me."

"Don't forget a Picasso worth millions."

She took another sip of her coffee and spoke over the rim of the cup. "The painting was an afterthought. A brilliant one, though, don't you think?"

"If you wanted to fake a kidnapping to disappear, why involve me? You obviously know Laporta quite well. How come he didn't realize his thug had snatched the wrong person?"

"I first met Señor Laporta last night. He was following orders from his employer. He had no idea we staged the kidnapping."

"We? You and Carlos Perella?"

"Me and Rafael Perella, Carlos's son. Rafael is my lover."

The plot thickened, but I still had many unanswered questions. "Were you really at Parc Güell yesterday?"

"Yes. I saw you wandering around the grounds and realized immediately that we might have a problem. Balaguer only had a headshot of me, and from the neck up, we look very similar."

A diplomatic way of saying that from the neck down no one could possibly mistake my pear-shaped excess booty for her size two figure.

"I saw Balaguer walk out with you," she continued, "but I couldn't exactly stop him to say he had the wrong victim."

"He might have killed me."

"He was instructed not to harm you."

"Your husband claimed you were in the room with him when he received Laporta's call."

Elaine scowled. "The bastard lied."

"Didn't he run a risk of the kidnappers harming you?"

"Michael is all about having the upper hand in negotiations. He wouldn't care that he risked my life by hanging up on Señor Laporta. It's all about winning with him. That's when I decided to up the ransom to include his precious painting."

There was still more that made no sense. "The police know Balaguer and Laporta abducted me. I picked them both out from mug shots. They'll go after them for kidnapping you. Aren't you worried your plan will backfire?"

"Your case has been dropped because you won't be around to testify."

"How do you know that?"

She smiled. "Do you think police corruption is something only found in the States?"

"That still doesn't absolve them of your kidnapping."

"Both have ironclad alibis for last night." She glanced at the watch on her wrist. "And by now Señor Perella has made a very generous contribution to the Barcelona police pension fund."

"That won't stop your husband from going after them."

"No, but this will." She withdrew a white business envelope from one of her jacket pockets and handed it to me. "This is what you will give my husband when you return without me."

The sealed envelope was devoid of any markings. I placed it on the table next to my coffee cup. "What does it say?"

"That I know where the bodies are buried, should he dare come after me or the people who helped me."

"*Literal* bodies?"

Instead of answering my question, she graced me with a Mona Lisa smile, then said, "You should finish your frittata while it's still hot."

Having lost my appetite, I placed my fork on the plate and grabbed my glass of sangria, polishing off the wine in an attempt to stave off the rage building within me. Instead of calming me, the sweet fruity alcohol fueled my anger. "You used me," I said. Worst of all, by drawing me into her scheme to defraud her husband, she'd ruined my Barcelona getaway.

"Not intentionally. It's not my fault Balaguer grabbed you instead of me, and I had no idea you'd show up at the museum last night. I merely took advantage of an opportunity that presented itself."

I slammed my empty glass onto the table. "I was tear gassed! Do you have any idea what that feels like?"

She shook her head. "I'm sorry. I didn't know about the tear gas. What can I do to make it up to you?"

I pushed back my chair and stood. "Look, I'm really sorry you're married to an abusive control freak. I know what it's like to discover your husband isn't the man you thought you'd married. But you had no right to drag me into your drama. What if something had gone wrong? Those men had guns."

"They were instructed not to harm anyone. They fired into the ceiling."

"Thugs don't always follow orders. Besides, bullets can ricochet. You have no idea what it was like in there with the room filling with tear gas and not even the emergency lights to guide us to safety. People panicked. Some were trampled in the dark and injured. Someone could have died. You risked my life and the lives of everyone else at that museum last night."

To my surprise her eyes filled with tears. "None of that was supposed to happen. I just wanted to get away from Michael and make him pay for the way he's treated me."

I picked up the envelope and dropped it into my purse. "I'll deliver the letter for you because I really have no other choice. Your husband is expecting me to secure your release. I need some explanation as to why that's not happening, and I doubt he'd believe me. He already thinks I'm somehow involved in your *kidnapping*."

"Thank you. I'll make it up to you. I promise."

"Unless you have a way of turning back time, that's not going to happen. Just get someone to bring me back to my hotel."

Elaine picked up her napkin and dabbed at her eyes. "Of course."

At that moment I heard what sounded like a helicopter off in the distance and approaching fast. The noise grew to deafening proportions as it hovered overhead. Had Michael Naiman planted another bug that Laporta overlooked? How far would Naiman go to drag his wife back? Would his men in black drop down on us, guns blazing? I looked up and held my breath.

Elaine stood. "That's my ride." Señor Laporta will return you to Barcelona." As if on cue, Laporta arrived, carrying two large suitcases that I assumed contained her clothes and all those diamonds from last night, perhaps much more. Someone probably entered her home and packed for her while we were all at the museum.

Elaine grabbed hold of the portfolio. I followed them both out to the back of the house where the helicopter landed in the middle of an expansive lawn. The pilot stepped out, grabbed the luggage and portfolio, and stored them inside the chopper.

Elaine took both my hands in hers and kissed me on both cheeks, European style. "Once again, thank you," she shouted into my ear over the roar of the rotors. "I hope at some point you can find it in your heart to forgive me for dragging you into this mess."

She stood back and our eyes locked. It might take a while, but I probably would forgive her. Her bruises spoke volumes as to the hell she'd lived through with Michael Naiman. I nodded. She smiled, turned, and headed for the chopper.

SIX

Laporta and I watched as the helicopter carrying Elaine rose into the air, then headed east. "Come, Señora Pollack, I will return you to Barcelona."

He led me back through the house and out the front door to his waiting Mercedes. As we got underway, I took out my phone. By now Zack would be frantic. Laporta reached across the seat, grabbed the phone from my hand, and slipped it into his breast pocket. "Not until I drop you off, *por favor*."

We drove in silence for most of the return trip, one that took far less time than the drive to the villa. Within an hour we arrived in the center of Barcelona. "If you don't mind, Señora, I will drop you off at Plaça de Catalunya."

"That's fine." I understood his hesitation to pull up in front of the hotel. Neither of us knew who'd be waiting there—Naiman, the police, or both. For his own protection Laporta couldn't risk being seen dropping me off at the hotel. Cars, trucks, and tourist buses circled the plaza. Street vendors, residents, and tourists jammed the area. No one would notice me stepping out of his car, especially if he parked on the side of the plaza farthest from the hotel.

He pulled up to the curb on a street across from the plaza and handed my phone back to me. I stared at him for a moment, waiting for him to say something, but he just clicked the door locks open, reached across the seat, and opened the passenger door. I unfastened my seatbelt and stepped out onto the curb. He nodded once after I closed the door before he pulled back into traffic and drove off.

I powered up my phone and checked for messages. Zack had called half a dozen times. Instead of listening to the messages, I called him.

He answered on the first ring. "Are you all right? Where the hell are you?"

"I'm at Plaça de Catalunya, and I'm fine."

"I didn't know what to think. You had me crazy with worry."

"I couldn't use my phone. I'll tell you everything as soon as I get to the hotel."

"The police are here. And Naiman."

"I figured as much."

"Is Elaine with you?"

I took a deep breath before I answered. "No. It's complicated. Don't say anything to Naiman."

"Okay."

I hung up, crossed the street, and cut through the plaza. The sun blazed overhead; a slight breeze whipped through my hair. Zack and I should be out enjoying the city on such a gorgeous afternoon. Instead, I expected to spend the remainder of the day being cross examined by Michael Naiman and debriefed by the police. At least I no longer had the feeling someone followed me.

As I approached the hotel, I counted three police cars parked in front of the building. The moment I stepped inside the lobby Naiman accosted me, two of his men in black close behind him. "Where's Elaine? Why isn't she with you?"

"Elaine is safe," I said.

"I don't believe you. You're involved in this. I've known it all along." He reached out and grabbed my wrist, squeezing so hard that I could feel the bruises forming.

"Let go of her," said Zack.

"Not until she tells me what she's done with my wife." He started shaking me. His goons stole a glance at each other, then stepped back as the half dozen policemen milling around the lobby drew closer, their hands resting on their guns but not interceding on my behalf.

Zack tried to pull Naiman away from me, but when he refused to release his grip, Zack landed a punch squarely on his jaw. Naiman stumbled backwards, pulling me along with him. Zack yanked me free as Naiman fell flat on his back.

He zeroed in on his bodyguards. "Don't just stand there gaping! Help me up!"

When neither stepped forward to offer him a hand, he rolled to his knees and leveraged himself off the marble floor. His entire body shook with rage, his face growing purple. "I'll deal with the two of you later." Then he pointed one of his pudgy fingers at Zack and screamed at the policemen, "I want that man arrested for assault!"

I held out my arm for all to see. Red marks encircled my wrist. "You assaulted me!"

He ignored me, instead turning to the nearest policeman. "I

want them both arrested. Now! Or I'll have your badges."

His standard threat to law enforcement, apparently. Michael Naiman was used to people jumping the moment he snapped his fingers. No one jumped, and that infuriated him even more. Veins bulged in his neck. His eyes narrowed, and he took a step toward me. That's when the police finally went into action, grabbing him before he got any closer.

"I've had enough," I said. I reached into my purse, withdrew Elaine's envelope, and handed it to one of the policemen. "This is from his wife. It will explain everything. I'm going up to my room. Please tell Captain De la Riva I'll stop by later to brief him on what happened and pick up my passport."

I turned and headed for the elevator. Zack followed. As the doors closed behind us, we heard Naiman roar. "I guess he read Elaine's letter," I said.

After Zack and I spent some much-needed alone time together and I filled him in on everything that had happened after he left for Parc Güell, we headed over to the police station to retrieve our passports.

De la Riva led us into his office and offered us seats. He informed us that he'd read Elaine's letter and that we were no longer persons of interest. "I'm sorry for your less-than-enjoyable stay in our city, Señora Pollack." He opened his top desk draw, withdrew our passports and handed them to us. "Perhaps you'll return in the future and see Barcelona as it is meant to be seen."

"Perhaps." Although highly unlikely unless some overly generous leprechaun decided to grace me with a pot of gold.

"We need to discuss Señor Naiman," he said.

"Why?"

"He claims you abetted in the theft of his painting." He turned to Zack. "And that you, Señor Barnes, assaulted him." The chief shrugged his shoulders. "However, we cannot seem to find any witnesses to corroborate his claims."

"Six of your officers and two of his own men witnessed him attack me," I said.

"That is my understanding. Do you wish to press charges? Señor Naiman is currently residing in one of our holding cells."

"I think Señor Naiman will suffer much more from his wife's actions than any sentence he'd receive for assault."

"And the Picasso?"

"His wife has the painting."

"Being his wife, that would make her half owner. Therefore, I see that no crime has been committed." He rose and extended his hand. "Have a safe trip home."

EPILOGUE

A week after our return from Barcelona, I arrived home from work to find a FedEx envelope addressed to me from a bank in Switzerland. Inside I found a note from Elaine Naiman.

Dear Anastasia,

I hope this letter finds you well. Although I realize you were never a willing participant, I wanted to thank you once again for helping me in my escape from Michael. The situation became far more complicated than I ever anticipated, and I'm sorry you were drawn into the drama.

During our conversation over brunch, you alluded to having your own marital problems. I asked Señor Perella to check with some of his associates in the States and learned that your husband left you deeply in debt. I hope the enclosed check will both help you pay off some of that debt and compensate you for the trouble I caused.

With deepest appreciation,
Elaine Naiman

I reached into the envelope and withdrew a second piece of paper, a bank check for twenty-five thousand dollars.

PATCHWORK PERIL

ONE

I glanced through the windshield at the ominous black sky. Accuweather called for a Nor'easter to hit within the hour. The brooding cloud cover suggested otherwise. With the rate the wind had begun to pick up, I figured I had three minutes tops to arrive home before a deluge of Diluvial proportions. A minute later the first large drops of rain splashed onto my windshield. By the time I turned down my street, sideway sheets of rain buffeted my car.

I pulled into my driveway, parked the car, opened the door, and darted for my back porch. That's when I caught a glimpse of bright colors frenetically flapping above the azalea bushes that separated my backyard from the one directly behind my house. Rosalie Schneider's award-winning patchwork quilts clung precariously to her clothesline. At any moment the gale force winds would sweep them off to parts unknown. The crafter in me couldn't let that happen.

With one quilt already hanging by a single clothespin, I had no time to grab my Wellingtons from the mudroom. I sandwiched my purse between my back door and storm door, then raced across the yard. Thick muck oozed up from the grass, sucking my shoes off my feet.

Welcome to the life of Anastasia Pollack, where no good deed goes unpunished.

By the time I reached Rosalie's clothesline and bundled the three waterlogged quilts into my arms, I was drenched from head to stocking-covered toes and spattered up to my armpits in mud. The quilts hadn't fared much better.

Huddled under the overhang, I banged on her back door. No one answered. I tried listening for some signs of activity inside the house, but the wind and rain drowned out all other sounds. Rosalie probably couldn't hear me. Shivering from the icy rain, I slogged my way back across both yards. As I bent to scoop up my now ruined Nine West pumps, I imagined my elderly neighbor, warm and cozy, curled up in front of her television, oblivious to my heroism on her behalf.

But if Rosalie were home, why hadn't she brought her quilts in before the storm hit?

"Holy cow, Mom!" Alex stood in the kitchen, Ralph, our Shakespeare quoting African Grey parrot on his shoulder. Both stared bug-eyed at me as I dropped the quilts, my shoes, and purse onto the mudroom floor. "What happened to you?"

"I was searching for Noah's ark."

Ralph squawked. "*There is, sure, another flood toward, and these couples are coming to the ark. As You Like It.* Act Five, Scene Four."

"Huh?" Alex ignored Ralph and directed his confusion toward me.

"Never mind. Please get my bathrobe for me."

When he returned, I closed the door separating the mudroom

from the kitchen, stripped down to my undies, and slipped on my robe. Before heading to a hot shower, I brought my clothes and Rosalie's quilts down to the basement. Those quilts would need washing before the mud stains set. Three more loads of wash to add to my Friday night chores. My punishment for being a nice neighbor was multiplying exponentially.

Back in the kitchen, I tried calling Rosalie but got her answering machine. Maybe she'd gone out to dinner with friends. I left a message telling her I had her quilts.

As I headed to my bedroom, Nick poked his head out from the room he shared with his brother. "Hi, Mom. What's for dinner?"

"Mud pies."

He plucked a twig from my hair and handed it to me. "I'll take mine with a side of bark."

"You've got it." Sarcasm is high on my list of flaws, one my teenage sons inherited from me, along with their honesty, integrity, sense of justice, and ability to score high grades. You can't have everything, right? Luckily, all they inherited from their father was his good looks. I'm clueless about their athletic ability. Those genes must have lain dormant for generations.

My weekend off to a stellar start, I locked myself in my bathroom, finished stripping off my remaining clothes, and stepped into the shower. Rivulets of mud and muck streamed from my body and swirled down the drain. If only all my problems washed away so easily.

~*~

By the next morning the fast-moving storm had traveled up into New England, and a bright autumn sun streamed through the windows. An unfamiliar quiet blanketed my normally chaos-filled home.

Alex and Nick had risen early to leave for a two-week all-school community service project, helping Habitat for Humanity build new homes for Hurricane Sandy victims. Mama now lived in a condo two miles away with her sixth husband and Catherine the Great, her portly Persian cat.

Lucille, my semi-invalid communist mother-in-law, was probably off fomenting a revolution somewhere with the twelve other members of the Daughters of the October Revolution. I hadn't seen her since yesterday morning. Apparently, she'd taken Manifesto (AKA Mephisto, AKA Devil Dog,) with her, because I hadn't seen the grumpy French bulldog since Friday morning, either. As long as Lucille didn't get herself arrested again, I really didn't care where she was or what she was doing. With any luck, she'd stay away all weekend.

I wasn't used to having the house to myself. Well, myself and a Shakespeare-quoting parrot. Too bad Zack was off either shooting indigenous flora and fauna with his Nikon or terrorists with his bad-ass Sig Sauer. (My boyfriend claims he's a photojournalist; I think he's a spy.)

I still hadn't heard from Rosalie Schneider. Her freshly laundered quilts sat folded on my dining room table. After breakfast I called her, only to have her answering machine pick up again. Had she gone away for the weekend and forgotten she left her quilts hanging on the line? To my knowledge she'd never exhibited any lapses of memory, but she was pushing eighty-five.

I decided to check to see if her car was parked in front of her house or in her garage, but I took the long way around the block rather than trudging through both soggy backyards.

In its wake, the storm had left a crisp breeze, enormous puddles, and a multitude of fallen branches throughout the neighborhood. Luckily, my property had sustained no damage, only a yard full of debris to clean up. Given my precarious finances, the last thing I needed was a huge repair bill. As I walked down the street, I realized some of my neighbors hadn't fared as well. An uprooted tree leaned against the roof of one house on the next block. Another tree had crushed two cars parked on the street.

When I arrived at Rosalie's house, I found her car parked in her driveway. I tried both her doors, ringing the front doorbell and knocking on the back door. Once again no one answered. However, this time I heard the television blaring from her living room. A sense of foreboding shuddered through my body. Ignoring the backyard muck, I kicked off my shoes and raced home to phone the police.

"9-1-1. State your emergency."

I quickly explained the reason for my call and rattled off Rosalie's address. "She's quite elderly. You need to send someone right away."

"Are you certain she's in the house, ma'am? Did you see her lying on the floor?"

"No, but—"

"Many people leave their televisions on to fool would-be burglars into thinking someone is home. It's also possibly she just didn't hear you. She may have been in the bathroom."

"Or she's injured and can't get to the door."

"I'll dispatch an officer as soon as possible, ma'am, but it will take time."

"Are you kidding me? A woman could be dying."

"No officers are available right now. Have you seen what's going on in town? We've got ruptured gas mains and downed power lines all over the place."

"And an elderly woman who may be in need of medical attention."

"You might want to see if any neighbors have a key to her house. Or get in touch with one of her relatives."

If Rosalie were going to give anyone a key to her home, I was the candidate-of-choice. Since I didn't have a key, I knew no one would. Rosalie didn't get along with either of her next-door neighbors. She and I had bonded over crafts when I moved into my house years ago and one day spied her quilts flapping in the breeze.

As for relatives, as far as I knew, there was only a niece living somewhere in the Midwest. Rosalie mentioned her once years ago when I asked about her family. Then she abruptly changed the subject.

"Just get someone there as soon as possible, please." With that I hung up. Maybe I was panicking over nothing, but my gut told me something was seriously wrong, and I needed to do something.

After pocketing my cell phone, I headed down the basement to grab a hammer and screwdriver. Then without bothering to wash the grass and mud from my feet, I stepped into my Wellingtons, traipsed back across the soggy yard, and squeezed through the azalea hedge.

Once at Rosalie's back door, I tried to jimmy the screwdriver in-between the door and the jamb, hoping I could pop the lock. When that didn't work, I looked around for some other way to get into the house.

The kitchen window seemed the likeliest candidate. If I could get enough leverage by standing on Rosalie's picnic table, I might be able to jimmy it open and climb through. If not, I'd have to resort to breaking the glass with the hammer.

Moving the picnic table proved extremely difficult. One of those old redwood varieties popular back in the middle of the last century, it weighed a ton. Pushing and pulling no more than an inch or two with each shove, I finally maneuvered it under the window. My arms and legs shook from the exertion, but I couldn't take time to recover. I grabbed the screwdriver and climbed onto the table.

Much to my surprise, the window was unlocked. I slid the pane open, and attempted to hoist myself up, not an easy task, given my disdain for any form of strenuous physical exercise, a fact made obvious by my slightly overweight, pear-shaped body. On my third attempt I gained enough purchase to swing one leg through the window—right into a sink of dirty dishes.

At that moment I knew something was definitely wrong with Rosalie Schneider. An obsessive-compulsive neat freak, she'd never leave a single dirty dish unwashed for longer than five minutes.

I scrambled out of the sink and grabbed a dishtowel to wipe down my boots. Rosalie would have a fit if I left footprints of mud and mashed potatoes all over her pristine hardwood floors.

"Rosalie?" I called her name as I made my way into the dining room. The last thing I wanted to do was give the woman a heart attack—assuming she hadn't already had one. She didn't answer.

Rosalie lived in an expanded Cape Cod-style house with a living room, dining room, kitchen, two bedrooms, and a bathroom on the first floor, plus two additional bedrooms and another bathroom on the second floor. As I walked through the dining room into the living room, I yelled louder, "Rosalie? It's Anastasia. Are you all right?"

I poked my head into the downstairs bedroom she used as her

quilting room, the other bedroom, and the bathroom. I then made my way upstairs. No Rosalie anywhere. Back in the living room, I grabbed the remote from her coffee table and switched off the Home Shopping Network.

By now dread had settled into every corpuscle of my body. The only place left to look was the basement. I headed back into the kitchen and opened the door leading to the basement stairs. Rosalie law sprawled and unmoving at the bottom of the steps.

TWO

I raced down the stairs, dropped to my knees, and felt for a pulse. My medical training didn't extend much beyond taking temperatures, doling out Tylenol, and kissing booboos, but eventually my probing fingers found a weak pulse in Rosalie's neck. At least she was alive. For now. But her gray pallor and the gash to her head, suggested she wouldn't last long without medical intervention.

Given the dishes in the sink, I suspected Rosalie had fallen last night right after dinner. An empty laundry basket lay upturned on the concrete floor a few feet from her body. She'd probably seen the storm approaching as she began to wash her dinner dishes, gone to the basement for the laundry basket, and fallen on her way back upstairs—either from tripping, fainting, or something far more serious.

I whipped out my phone and called 9-1-1 again. Since I'd actually found Rosalie injured and in need of immediate medical attention, I was taken more seriously this time and was told an ambulance was on its way. One arrived in less than five minutes.

While the two paramedics worked on her, one of them asked me to locate her purse. The hospital would need her ID, insurance, and Medicare cards. I found the purse hanging in her downstairs coat closet and handed it to one of the men after they'd loaded Rosalie into the ambulance. Then I raced home to grab my own purse to follow them to the hospital.

Not an easy task, considering all the downed trees and power lines scattered throughout town. The more I inched my way around detours and through intersections without working traffic lights, the more I realized how much my neighbors and I had dodged a gale force bullet.

Thousands of people throughout the area had no power. Many had crushed cars and damage to their homes from all the felled trees and broken limbs. The Nor'easter hadn't lasted more than a few hours, and although not nearly the caliber of Superstorm Sandy, the destruction, at least in some areas, came in a close second.

The normally fifteen-minute drive to the hospital took me nearly an hour. Hopefully, the ambulance had made better time. In hindsight, I probably shouldn't have bothered making the trip. Privacy laws would prevent the staff from divulging any details of Rosalie's condition to me. Obviously, I wasn't thinking clearly when I jumped in my car. However, since I was there, maybe someone would at least tell me if she'd survive.

I gave my name to the woman behind the information desk in the emergency room. "An ambulance brought Mrs. Rosalie Schneider in a little while ago."

The admissions clerk glanced up from her computer screen and peered at me through an enormous pair of octagonal, red-framed glasses that clashed against a head of over-processed orange frizz. Her ID badge gave her name as Willow Krause, a name completely at odds with the woman sitting behind the glass partition. Bordering on obese, Willow Krause was anything but a willow. "Are you a relative?" she asked.

"No, I'm—"

She stopped me mid-sentence to rattle off hospital policy.

"Mrs. Schneider has a niece who should be notified," I said. Someone needed to advocate for Rosalie. Not that I knew her wishes, but an unconscious woman certainly couldn't make decisions regarding her own medical care.

"Do you have contact information for her?"

"No, she lives somewhere in the Midwest, I believe. I don't even know her name."

"No local family?"

"None that I know of."

The woman turned her attention to her keyboard and began typing. "I see we have Mrs. Schneider's records from a previous admission last year. Her niece's phone number is listed. We'll contact her." Then she dismissed me by summoning the next person queued up in the waiting room.

I took the none-too-subtle hint. As I exited the hospital, I braced myself for the many detours awaiting me on my trip home.

~*~

I spent most of the remainder of the afternoon raking up storm debris, first on my property, then on Rosalie's. Someone had to do it, and crowds of volunteers weren't fighting each other for the honor of cleaning up Rosalie's yard.

After I finished, I showered and changed my clothes, then called the hospital, hoping for some information on Rosalie's condition. The woman on the other end of the line wouldn't tell me anything other than visiting hours ended at eight o'clock. I took that as a good sign and decided to forego more weekend chores in favor of paying Rosalie a visit.

~*~

The blinking and beeping equipment in Rosalie's room indicated she was still in a coma and not merely sleeping. I had convinced myself otherwise, that allowing visitors meant she'd awakened. My heart sank as I stood beside her bed and stared down at her.

She wore a cast on her right hand and wrist, another on her left foot, propped up on a pillow at the base of the bed. An IV tube snaked from a suspended drip bag into her left arm. Various wires ran from the machines and disappeared under the lightweight blanket draped over her frail body. Up until yesterday Rosalie could shave ten years off her age, and no one would question her. Today she looked every bit a mid-octogenarian and then some.

The door swooshed open, and a nurse entered to change the nearly empty IV bag. "Will she come out of it?" I asked.

She finished her task and turned to me. "The doctors are quite optimistic. You're her niece?"

"No, I'm the neighbor who discovered her."

The nurse frowned. "Oh. I really can't discuss her condition with you."

"I understand. Is her niece on the way?"

"We were told she'd arrive this afternoon." The nurse then hurried out of the room.

I pulled a chair up to Rosalie's bed, clasped her good hand, and settled in for a nonstop, one-way conversation. Somewhere I'd read talking to comatose patients helped them regain consciousness. Or maybe that was an old wives' tale. Either way, I figured it couldn't hurt.

Half an hour later, all talked out, I stood to leave. As I reached for the door handle, the door swung inward, and a corporate-looking woman with a Rubenesque figure entered the room. She wore a deep eggplant power suit over a celery green silk blouse and eggplant suede stilettos. Her shoulder-length ebony hair was tucked behind her ears, the better to show off diamond studs the equivalent of a year at Harvard. (Ever since Dead Louse of a Spouse gambled away our kids' college funds, I tend to see material possessions in terms of tuition payments.)

A thickly trowelled layer of makeup attempted—unsuccessfully—to disguise her age, which I pegged at somewhere north of fifty. Rosalie's brown Coach purse, along with a Louis Vuitton black leather tote, hung from her right shoulder. She dragged a rolling suitcase with the iconic LV logo behind her.

"You must be Rosalie's niece," I said, suddenly too aware of my bleach-stained jeans and faded *Defy Gravity* T-shirt.

She nodded. "And you are?"

"Anastasia Pollack. Rosalie's neighbor."

"The one who found her?"

"Yes."

She parked the suitcase and extended her hand. "Jane Sherman. My aunt is fortunate she has someone like you looking out for her."

"When was the last time you saw her?"

"We've never met."

"Oh?"

"Family feud going back before I was born."

"Yet you flew halfway across the country for her?"

She shrugged. "Obligation, I suppose. The two of us are all

that's left of the family. She'll probably toss me out on my rear the moment she wakes up."

"Must have been some feud."

Jane rolled her eyes before glancing toward the bed. "To look at her now, lying there so frail and pathetic, you'd never suspect the vindictive nature of the woman."

"Vindictive? Not the Rosalie Schneider I know." Although, she never had a kind word to say about either of her next-door neighbors, I found most of Rosalie's complaints justified. One neighbor's dogs barked constantly, and the other neighbor came and went at all hours of the night on a Hog that could be heard half a mile away.

"Perhaps she's mellowed with age. Anyway, there's no point hanging around here while she's still in a coma. I only stopped by for her keys so I can get into the house."

She spun on her heels and headed for the door but stopped and turned back before exiting. "Any chance I can hitch a ride to Westfield with you instead of calling a cab? It cost me a fortune to get here from the airport."

I couldn't really say no, could I? Besides, Jane had unleashed my curiosity gene. What had happened all those years ago to cause such bad blood between Rosalie and other members of her family? And given all that bad blood, why would she list her niece as the emergency contact on her hospital forms? Not that I wanted any more obligations in my life since I was already saddled with the communist mother-in-law from Hell, but I was certainly closer to Rosalie than this niece she'd never met.

However, Jane remained vague on details during the drive back to Westfield. I learned little other than she was single, worked in finance, and had a friend from college who'd moved to New Jersey a few years ago. "Basking Ridge," she said. "Is that anywhere near here?"

"About half an hour away."

"Excellent."

A few minutes later I pulled into Rosalie's driveway. "If you need anything, my house is directly behind this one. Rosalie has my number next to her phone in the kitchen."

"I'm sure I'll be fine. Thanks for the lift."

"How long do you plan to stay?"

"That all depends on Rosalie and whether or not she recovers."

"What about your job?"

She patted her tote. "As long as I have my computer, I can work anywhere."

~*~

Later that night I remembered Rosalie's quilts. The queen-size Wedding Ring, along with a twin Star of Bethlehem and a full-sized Dutchman's Puzzle still occupied a large section of my dining room table. I placed them in a heavy-duty plastic trash bag, slipped into my Wellies, and headed out the back door.

Light from Rosalie's kitchen cast a soft glow over her yard. As I approached the back door, I noticed two silhouettes through the white linen curtain covering the kitchen window. Jane's college friend must be visiting. Not wanting to intrude on the reunion, I decided to head back home and deliver the quilts another day.

THREE

Not that I had anything against her, but Jane struck me as someone who wouldn't spend time at the hospital, talking to a virtual stranger in a coma. For that reason, I felt obligated to visit Rosalie as often as possible. After dinner Monday night, I drove back to the hospital. With all the roads now clear and power restored, I made the trip in the usual fifteen minutes.

I found Rosalie propped up in bed. The gray pallor gone, she looked amazingly well for a woman who had tumbled down a flight of stairs, broken several bones, and fallen into a coma three days ago.

"I'm so happy to see you awake," I said.

She offered me a weak smile. "I don't know what happened."

"What was the last thing you remember?"

"Realizing I needed to grab the quilts off the clothesline before the rain started." She sighed. "I suppose they're ruined."

"No, they're sitting on my dining room table. Freshly laundered."

"Thank you so much." Her brow wrinkled. "You're...?"

"Anastasia. Your neighbor."

"Of course, dear. I'm sorry. Everything is so fuzzy."

"The doctors said Aunt Rosalie might experience some minor memory loss until her brain fully heals," said Jane, stepping out of the attached bathroom. She carried a vase filled with gold and russet mums that she placed on the windowsill.

"When will they release you?" I asked Rosalie.

Jane answered for her. "Possibly tomorrow."

"And you'll stay with her until she's fully recovered?"

"Of course."

"I can fend for myself," said Rosalie. "Always have, always will."

"With a broken wrist and ankle?" asked Jane.

"I'll manage."

Jane sighed. "Aunt Rosalie, whatever happened between you and my mother has nothing to do with me. She and my father have been gone for years. Don't you think it's time you moved on and we got to know each other?"

"Why?"

"Because we have no other family."

"And this just occurred to you? After how many years? If you're angling to inherit, you can forget it. With the exception of a few bequests, I'm leaving all my money to charity. And don't think you'll be able to contest the will. I was of totally sound mind when I signed it."

Jane waved her hand across her body. Today she wore a pair of navy wool crepe slacks paired with a muted gold silk oxford shirt and a classic Hermes scarf. The scarf alone cost more than my entire outfit. "Do I look like I need your money?" she asked.

Rosalie turned to me. "She just suddenly appeared out the

blue."

"The hospital called her," I said. "You listed her as your next of kin."

"Only because I had to. It was either give them her name or lie and say I had no family. I don't lie." She narrowed her gaze at Jane. "Unlike some people."

Jane's hand flew to her chest, and her lower lip quivered as she spoke. "I haven't lied to you."

"I'm not talking about you."

I placed my hand on Jane's arm. "Why don't you get a cup of coffee?"

She sniffed. "Maybe you can talk some sense into her while I'm gone. I only want what's best for her."

After she left the room, I pulled a chair up to Rosalie's bed. "Why the hostility?" I asked.

"How would you feel if you caught your husband cheating on you with your sister?"

About as well as I felt after learning my own husband cheated on me with Lady Luck, then left me penniless and saddled with his curmudgeon of a mother after he dropped dead in Las Vegas.

But Rosalie didn't know the details of my widowhood, and I meant to keep it that way from her and every other one of my neighbors. Gossip travels fast in a small town. "Is Jane a product of that affair?" I asked.

She nodded. "I wouldn't give the bastard a divorce. They never married. Or if they did, he was a bigamist on top of being a philanderer."

"Jane said her last name is Sherman. How did you even know about her?"

"My father hired a private investigator to track down Freddie and Norma—my husband and sister—after they ran off. Freddie had worked for my father. He not only ran off with Norma, he absconded with the week's payroll. The detective found them about a year later, living in Omaha under assumed names. Jane was already born by then. My father never told me."

"How did you find out?"

"I came across paperwork when I was settling his estate. He'd disowned Norma, but he set up a trust fund for Jane. That's how I had her contact information for the hospital."

I took her good hand in mine. "What your husband and sister did to you was terrible, Rosalie, but you can't blame Jane."

"I know it's not rational, but looking at her brings back all the hurt and betrayal. I never wanted to meet her. After more than half a century, the pain is as fresh as the day I walked in on them." She cringed. "Going at it like a couple of rutting sheep."

I suspected Jane's parents told their daughter a much different tale regarding her aunt. Jane had called Rosalie vindictive. Not that I didn't believe Rosalie, but perhaps the truth lay somewhere in-between. "Maybe you should give Jane a chance. You can't function on your own with casts on your arm and foot."

"I have friends."

"Most of whom are your age or older. Would any of them really be able to manage helping you bathe, dress, get to a doctor's appointment?"

Rosalie heaved a deep sigh and shook her head. "Doubtful."

"It's either Jane or hiring a home health aide."

She made a face. "I don't want strangers in my home."

"Jane isn't a stranger; she's family. Estranged family, but family all the same." Which is what I constantly remind myself whenever the urge strikes to strangle my mother-in-law.

"I'm a bitter, old woman who had her life stolen from her. I wanted children. Desperately. They took that from me." She spit out a sardonic laugh. "Do you realize in addition to being my niece, since Freddie and I never divorced, Jane is also my stepdaughter? How ironic is that?"

"It does sound like something out of a soap opera."

"I suppose I have no choice, do I?"

Before I could answer, Jane entered the room. She carried a cardboard take-out tray containing three cups. "I thought you might like some, too," she said, handing me one of the cups. Then she passed the remaining cup to Rosalie. "I brought you chamomile tea. It should help you sleep."

Rosalie scowled. "I've been asleep for three days." When she caught my frown, she added, "But thank you. That was very considerate."

"And?" I prompted her.

"And I also appreciate that you put your life on hold to fly here for me."

Jane's face lit up. "Thank you."

~*~

The hospital discharged Rosalie the next day. That evening, I walked through our respective backyards for a quick visit and to return Rosalie's quilts.

"The poor dear was exhausted," said Jane when she answered my knock at the back door. "She's already sound asleep. I'll let her know you stopped by."

I handed over the bag. "What's this?" she asked.

"The quilts I rescued from her clothesline the day she fell."

Jane scowled at the large plastic bag. "More? Every square inch of this place is covered with these rags."

Not everyone appreciates the craftsmanship that goes into quilting, but as an editor whose livelihood depends on crafts and crafters, I found Jane's comment offensive. "Rosalie's quilts have appeared in several museum exhibitions."

Jane shrugged. "No accounting for some people's taste, right?"

"Quite true." I looked her right in the eyes and added, "Some people have extremely poor taste." I then made an excuse about having to help my mother-in-law and took my leave.

~*~

Both Wednesday and Thursday I worked late and didn't have a chance to visit Rosalie. Friday evening, I arrived home to red and blue lights flashing through the azalea bushes.

FOUR

I raced through both yards to Rosalie's back door, which swung open at my first knock. Officers Fogarty and Harley, two of Westfield's finest, stood on the other side of the door. I had feared the worst but saw no evidence of a medical emergency. Rosalie sat at her kitchen table, no paramedics in sight. She glared daggers at Jane who stood in the middle of the room, arms folded in front of her chest, her lips pursed tightly together.

"What happened?" I asked.

Rosalie glared at Jane. "She's trying to kill me."

Was Jane mistreating her? Rosalie sported no fresh bruises, cuts, or scrapes, only the fading remnants of last week's accident. Her body was clean, her clothing laundered, her silver hair recently washed and pulled back into a neat bun at the nape of her neck.

"How was I to know she's allergic to shellfish?" asked Jane. "She never told me not to buy certain foods."

Rosalie showed no evidence of an allergic reaction, no hives, no swelling, no difficulty breathing. "Did you eat any shellfish?" I asked her.

"Of course not! The moment I saw the empty can of clam sauce sitting on the counter, I called the police."

I turned to the officers, both of whom were veterans of countless run-ins with my cantankerous mother-in-law. "I think this is all a big misunderstanding."

"That's what we've been trying to tell Mrs. Schneider," said Harley, a heavy-set man in his fifties and the senior of the two officers.

"But she's demanding we arrest Miss Sherman for attempted murder," added Fogarty, the junior partner by about ten years.

I sighed. "Really, Rosalie?"

Her belligerent attitude dissolved, replaced by one of confusion. She stared at the quilted placemat in front of her, picking at a loose thread. "Something is not right," she mumbled.

"With your attitude," said Jane.

Rosalie raised her head. The confusion dissolved. Her features hardened as she glared at Jane.

Researchers now believe that head trauma can cause dementia years later. As the mother of sons who play sports, I worried constantly about concussions and knew to look for certain symptoms after a blow to the head. Had the hospital released Rosalie too soon? I settled into the chair next to her and placed my hand on her forearm. "Are you nauseous, Rosalie?"

She pulled her attention from Jane, her features softening as she turned to me. "No."

"Dizzy?"

"No."

"Do you have a headache? Ringing in the ears? Blurred vision?

Further memory loss?"

She denied suffering from any symptoms.

"She's not telling you the truth," said Jane. "She's extremely forgetful. She's constantly accusing me of stealing things, but I'll find the items she claims I stole in different rooms. In plain view. What happens when I go home? Will she forget to turn off the stove and burn the house down?"

Could severe head trauma cause sudden dementia? I had no idea. "Maybe you should bring her to the hospital for a scan," I said to Jane.

"I don't think that's necessary. The doctors warned me she might experience further bouts of memory loss, along with possible confusion or emotional instability."

"For how long?"

"Anywhere from days to months."

"Months?"

"No one really knows for sure. Her brain is still healing."

"I'm not delusional," said Rosalie. "She's trying to make you think I'm crazy."

Jane ignored her. "She must have called the police while I was in the bathroom." She came up behind Rosalie and patted her shoulder. "I'm sure she'll be fine in the morning. "All she needs is a pill and a good night's sleep."

"What kind of pill?" I asked.

"The doctor prescribed a mild anti-anxiety medication to take as needed. I'll get one for her."

While she was gone, I tried to convince Rosalie that Jane hadn't tried to kill her. "She's gone out of her way to help you, Rosalie. What would she have to gain by killing you? She's not after your money."

"So she says."

"She knows you have an ironclad will. Can we let the officer's leave now?"

"I suppose." She glanced across the room to where Harley and Fogarty both leaned their massive frames against the kitchen counter, one on either side of the sink. "I'm sorry. Maybe I did overreact."

"Don't worry about it, ma'am," said Harley. "We'll chalk it up to your recent injury."

I walked the two officers to the front door. When I returned to the kitchen, Rosalie's stomach rumbled loud enough to startle me. "When did you last eat?" I asked.

She glanced at the wall clock. "Lunch, I suppose. Why can't I remember?"

"Because you're still healing," said Jane, returning to the kitchen. She placed a small pink pill in front of Rosalie, then filled a glass with tap water and handed it to her.

I swung open the refrigerator door and pulled out a loaf of bread and packages of deli ham and sliced cheddar. "How about a sandwich?"

"I'll make it," said Jane. "I'm sure you have your own dinner to prepare, Anastasia."

She took the food packages from me and placed them on the counter. Then she turned her attention back to Rosalie who sat staring at the pill on the table. "Take your medicine, Aunt Rosalie. You'll feel better. Then we'll have a nice chat about any other allergies you have."

~*~

Rosalie called me the next day. "Would you mind coming over? I'd like your help with something."

"I'll be right there."

"Bring your camera."

My camera? That seemed like an odd request, but I grabbed it out of my work tote before leaving the house.

Rosalie met me at her back door. "Where's Jane?" I asked.

"Out."

"Running errands?"

"I'm not sure what she's doing, but she's up to no good."

"Rosalie, we've been through this."

"Sit down, and hear me out." With the aid of one crutch and her good arm, she hobbled over to the kitchen table and settled into a chair. When I took the chair opposite her, she continued, "I've been feeling muddleheaded ever since the hospital discharged me."

"That's understandable."

"No. Not like this. I'm sleeping all the time, and when I'm awake, I feel like my brain is full of cobwebs."

"Maybe your meds need to be adjusted."

"I stopped taking them. And I didn't eat the breakfast Jane prepared for me this morning,. I think she's drugging me."

As far as I knew, Rosalie had never suffered from paranoia. This change in her personality might be a result of the fall or a side effect of her medication. "Why would she do that?"

"That's what I want you to find out. Last night when she placed that pill in front of me, I experienced a moment of clarity. As if something had cut a path through all those cobwebs. I pretended to take the pill. This morning, when she left the kitchen, I tossed my breakfast down the drain. And do you know what?"

I shook my head.

"I don't feel muddleheaded today. Not one bit. But I pretended otherwise, same as I did last night."

"Did something happen after I left last night?"

"When she thought I was asleep, she left the house."

"For how long?"

"Hours. I tried staying awake, but I finally fell asleep around two o'clock. This morning I pleaded exhaustion after breakfast. Twenty minutes after I pretended to doze off, she left again."

I studied Rosalie and saw the exact same woman I knew prior to her tumble down the basement stairs. Sane. Rational. But was she?

"There's more," she said. "Things keep disappearing."

"Jane said she found the items you claimed were missing."

"Jane is playing games. That's why I asked you to bring your camera. I want you to take pictures to document where everything is in each room. I also want you to find those pills she's been giving me. I looked in the downstairs bathroom. They're not there. She probably has them hidden upstairs."

At this point, I didn't know what or whom to believe, but I had nothing to lose by humoring Rosalie. We went room by room throughout her downstairs as she pointed out various pieces of bric-a-brac, vases, china, and jewelry she wanted me to document. All hardly worth stealing. Besides, judging from Jane's designer wardrobe, I doubt she'd be caught dead with any of Rosalie's possessions.

"The quilts, too," she said. "She keeps eyeing them."

Rosalie need not have worried about Jane stealing her quilts. I didn't have the heart to tell her what Jane thought of her handiwork. I kept my mouth firmly shut and dutifully shot photos of each quilted wall-hanging, table runner, pillow, and blanket throughout the downstairs rooms.

After quilting for over fifty years, Rosalie had amassed enough of a collection to open her own quilt shop. She rarely sold or gave away any of her quilts. However, she occasionally donated one for a local charity auction. When she did, the winning bids ran into the thousands of dollars. Throughout the area, a Rosalie Schneider quilt was highly prized, not just for the quality of her workmanship, but also because so few people were lucky enough to own one.

I spent nearly an hour capturing images of every quilt on the first floor. When I finished, Rosalie said, "You'll have to go upstairs by yourself. I can't manage the steps with these casts."

"Do you want me to photograph anything upstairs besides the quilts?"

"No, just find those pills."

In the upstairs bathroom medicine cabinet, I found a container of Xanax. I brought the pills down to Rosalie. "The prescription is in your name. A quarter milligram, three times a day. I believe that's a very low dose."

She held out her good hand. "Let me see what they look like."

I popped open the cap and spilled a white pill into her palm. "These aren't the pills she's been giving me."

"The pill Jane gave you last night—"

"Was pink. I told you she's drugging me."

Up until this point I'd dismissed all of Rosalie's rants about Jane, convinced she was projecting her long-held anger toward her husband and sister onto Jane. Now I began to have doubts. "What about the other pills she gave you? Were they all pink?"

Rosalie thought for a minute, then shook her head. "I can't remember. I was clearheaded when I left the hospital, then everything grew muddled until this morning."

"What do you want me to do, Rosalie?"

"I want you to call the police. They won't believe me, not after last night."

I doubted they'd take me seriously, either. If Rosalie were as befuddled as she claimed the last few days, her memory would be far from reliable. As for the pills, I knew of a simple way to find some answers.

I headed into the kitchen, grabbed Rosalie's phone, and punched in the number for the pharmacy. When the pharmacist came on the line, I placed the phone on speaker. "I'm calling for Mrs. Rosalie Schneider. She's a bit confused by her medications. Can you explain to her what she was prescribed since Tuesday?"

After he verified that Rosalie was with me, he said, "Certainly. One moment while I access your records, Mrs. Schneider." Computer keys clicked in the background. "Here we are. On Tuesday we filled a prescription for Xanax and Tylenol with codeine. Last night your doctor called in a lesser dosage of Xanax. The original prescription was for a half milligram. The new prescription is for a quarter milligram."

"What color are the Xanax?" I asked.

"The half milligram pills are pink; the quarter milligrams are white."

Mystery solved. I thanked the pharmacist and hung up. "Rosalie, I believe Jane noticed how muddled you've been and called the doctor to adjust your medication. She left last night to pick up the new prescription."

"Then explain why she gave me a pink pill this morning."

I couldn't. "Are you sure?"

Rosalie hesitated. Confusion settled over her face. "I think so."

"What did you do with this morning's pill?"

"I flushed it down the toilet."

"Since we have no way of proving which pill you were given, why don't we give Jane the benefit of the doubt and wait to see which pill she gives you later?"

"But she was gone for hours last night. The pharmacy is less than a mile away."

"Is it possible you dozed off and didn't hear her come back?" Or more likely Rosalie was still suffering from the effects of too high a dose of Xanax and had no real concept of time, but I refrained from suggesting that possibility.

"So where is she now? Explain that. She left the house at nine-thirty." Rosalie glanced up at the clock mounted on her kitchen wall. "It's almost noon."

Jane wasn't hired help. However, if she had decided to take off for a few hours, she should have told Rosalie. "Have you had anything to eat today?"

"Some toast and an apple after she left this morning. I couldn't manage more than that."

I set about preparing her a sandwich. Jane walked in as Rosalie took her first bite. "Aunt Rosalie, I'm so sorry! I had no idea the dentist would take so long."

"You were at the dentist?" I asked.

Jane looked from me to Rosalie. "Don't you remember?"

"You never mentioned anything about a dentist."

Jane turned to me. "I broke a tooth last night after you left. Rosalie gave me the name of her dentist. I called first thing this morning. He squeezed me in for an emergency appointment." She turned back to Rosalie. "You don't remember our conversation this morning before you went back to bed?"

Rosalie dropped her sandwich onto her plate. Her eyes narrowed; her voice rose. "We never had a conversation about a broken tooth, and I didn't give you my dentist's name."

Jane shook her head and sighed. "Another lapse of memory," she said to me.

Then she turned back to Rosalie. "I spoke with your doctor last night after the police left. I've suspected your medication was too strong. When I told him about the forgetfulness and paranoia, he agreed with me and phoned in a prescription for a lower dose. I picked it up last night after you went to bed. Hopefully, we'll begin to see some improvement soon, although I'd hoped by now—"

Rosalie slammed her fist on the table. "I'm not paranoid."

Jane's phone rang. She fished it out of her purse and checked the display. "I have to take this," she said leaving the kitchen. "It's a business call."

FIVE

"She never said anything about going to the dentist," reiterated Rosalie once Jane was out of earshot.

I reminded her that she couldn't remember the color of the pill Jane had given her this morning. "Although you're no longer feeling muddleheaded, you still might be suffering side effects from the medication."

She reluctantly conceded.

After Jane finished her call and returned to the kitchen, I headed home. Jane had freely offered valid explanations for her absences from the house—without being asked. Rosalie exhibited definite personality changes, whether from her accident, her medications, or both. The logical side of my brain told me to dismiss Rosalie's claims. Yet, I'd known Rosalie for years, and I'd only met Jane a week ago. The emotional side of my brain urged me not to dismiss Rosalie's suspicions and accusations.

Or maybe her paranoia was rubbing off on me.

Out of curiosity, once back in my house, I fired up my

computer and searched "Xanax side effects." Some of the more common ones included forgetfulness, sleepiness, irritability, and trouble concentrating. A few of the less common side effects included changes in behavior and problems with memory. Rosalie had exhibited all of these symptoms to some extent, but they were also some of the symptoms associated with her injury.

Since Jane had given me no reason to question her behavior or motives, I allowed the logical side of my brain to win out over the emotional side. I powered down my computer and headed to the basement to toss in the first load of a week's worth of laundry.

A few minutes later, while transferring a sink full of dirty dishes into the dishwasher, I noticed Jane gingerly tiptoeing across my yard in an effort to avoid her stiletto heels sinking into the still-soft earth. I met her at the back door.

"Can we talk?" she asked.

I ushered her inside and offered her a cup of coffee. While I made a fresh pot, she took a seat at the kitchen table. "How do you put up with Rosalie?" she asked.

"I've had a lot of practice. You should meet my mother-in-law. But Rosalie isn't normally like this."

"Is it me or the results of the accident?"

"I've wondered about that."

"Any conclusions?"

"I think it may be a combination of both."

"Why is she so hostile toward me? I've gone out of my way to come here. I hardly knew anything about her before the hospital called me last week. I didn't even know she was still alive."

"What did you know?"

"Just that she was jealous of my mother and tried to break up my parents' marriage. They moved halfway across the country to get away from her."

I poured two cups of coffee, handed Jane one, and took the seat opposite her. "Rosalie tells a quite different story. She claims she was married to your father and caught him having sex with your mother."

Jane froze, her coffee cup halfway to her mouth. Her features hardened. "She's lying."

"She also said she never gave your father a divorce. Either he and your mother never married, or he was a bigamist."

"I don't believe it. The woman's delusional. My parents were honest, God-fearing people. They'd never do anything like that."

I shrugged. "Everyone has secrets. Maybe the truth lies somewhere in-between."

"Still, that's no reason for her to hate me. I had nothing to do with what happened."

"No, but Rosalie was trying to get pregnant when she claims to have walked in on your parents. Not only did they betray her, they stole her chance to have a child of her own. I imagine when she looks at you, she sees the daughter she never had."

Jane frowned but said nothing.

"Give her a chance," I continued. "Once she's fully recovered, the two of you might be able to forge a friendship. After all, neither of you has any other family."

"I'd like nothing better, but it's up to her."

~*~

Zack returned from his latest jaunt to find me on my hands and knees, scrubbing the kitchen floor. He looked like sex on a stick, even with his rumpled clothes and several days of stubble.

If he ever traced his DNA, I'm betting we'd discover his genetic material cavorted in the same gene pool with that of Pierce

Brosnan, Hugh Jackman, and Antonio Banderas. He's that good-looking. What he sees in me with my slightly overweight, pear-shaped body, is something I'll never understand, but I'm not complaining.

However, putting aside the pear-shape and extra pounds, I currently looked like crap. And probably smelled worse. "You might want to keep your distance until I've had time to shower," I said.

He sized me up, then pulled me to my feet and into his arms. "Compared to where I've been? I'll take my chances."

"And where might that be this time?"

"Cameroon."

"Do I want to know what's in Cameroon?"

"Eisentraut's Shrew."

Ralph, perched atop the refrigerator, flapped his wings and squawked. "*Is she so hot a shrew as she's reported? The Taming of the Shrew*. Act Four, Scene One."

Zack turned to Ralph. "Absolutely."

"We were discussing Cameroon, not Kate," I said. Or was he referring to me? I decided ignorance was bliss. "No militants, terrorists, or drug warlords in Cameroon?"

"Probably all three. But I was there for the shrews."

Of course he was. "What's so special about Eisentraut's Shrew?"

"It's endangered."

I'd Google that later. No matter how much he denies it, I still think Zack's photojournalism is a cover for his work as a government operative.

"Where is everyone?" he asked, changing the subject. "It's far too quiet in this house." Zack is very good at changing the subject whenever the subject is his work. Another reason I suspect he's not who he says he is, no matter how many photo credits and bylines he's amassed over the years.

"The boys are on a school service project, and Lucille took off early this morning with her fellow revolutionaries." I glanced at the clock. "So far I haven't received a call from the police, so I suppose she's staying out of trouble."

"Or hasn't been caught yet."

"Another possibility." And knowing Lucille, the more likely.

"I think we should take advantage of the situation."

"What are you suggesting?"

He twined his fingers with mine and led me through the dining room and living room, then down the hall toward my bedroom. However, instead of stopping at the bed, he continued into the bathroom. "You scrub my back, I'll scrub yours," he said.

Hopefully, *back* was a euphemism for other parts of our anatomy.

~*~

Sometime later, my rumbling stomach interrupted the hazy bliss of our sated bodies. I untangled my limbs from Zack's limbs and shifted to glance at the clock on my nightstand. Five-thirty. Nearly dinnertime. I hadn't eaten since breakfast.

"Sounds like I need to take you to dinner," said Zack.

"I can whip up something here." Or he could. Of the two of us, Zack was the gourmet cook.

He swung his legs off the side of the bed, stood, and stretched. "Let's go to Short Hills. I need to buy a birthday present for the twins. They turn three next week."

The twins, Mia and Chloe, belonged to Zack's ex-wife Patricia and her second husband. Zack and Patricia married too young, realized their mistake almost immediately, and parted friends. When Patricia's dormant maternal genes showed up a few years ago, she became a first-time mom in her early forties, and Zack became Uncle Zacky.

~*~

Twenty minutes later Zack maneuvered his silver Porshe Boxster around the winding curves of Watchung Reservation on our way to one of the most upscale malls in the country. Before Dead Louse of a Spouse had reduced me to pauperdom, I would occasionally splurge on an item at the Short Hills Mall. More often than not, though, I'd limit my shopping to Macy's with the rare foray into Nordstrom or Bloomingdale's. Even back then, when I was comfortably ensconced in the realm of the middleclass, I couldn't afford to shop in most of the mall's pricey designer boutiques.

I'd been to the mall twice since Karl died. The first time was last winter when the police coerced me into taking part in an unsuccessful sting to flush out Ricardo the loan shark.

A few months later I found myself back at the mall. Mama had wanted an appraisal for the engagement ring Lou Beaumont gave her prior to his murder. She walked into Tiffany & Co. flashing a diamond the size of Cleveland, never expecting the gemologist to take one look at the ring and sniff his disdain. Quintessential robin's egg blue box notwithstanding, Cleveland definitely didn't come from Tiffany's.

Needless to say, I had less than fond memories of my last two trips to the mall.

"Italian or seafood?" asked Zack as he pulled into the covered parking garage and began trolling for an empty spot.

"Whichever has the shortest wait time. I'm famished."

"We have a reservation at both. I made them while you were dressing. I'll cancel the one we don't use."

I opted for Italian. Although I loved the food at Legal Sea Foods, I preferred Papa Razzi's quieter ambiance for a romantic dinner for two.

Zack nosed into a parking space and killed the engine. "Those two look like they bought out the mall," he said, pointing to a couple of women one parking lane in front of us. They struggled to load dozens of shopping bags into the trunk of a car that looked suspiciously like Rosalie Schneider's gray Ford Escort, given the *Warning: I Brake for Quilt Shops* sticker on the rear bumper.

I placed my hand on Zack's thigh. "Don't get out of the car yet."

"Why? What's the matter?"

I waited until one of the women closed the trunk. Both still had several large shopping bags looped over their arms. And not just any shopping bags. These women hadn't spent their money at Macy's or even Bloomingdale's. Their shopping bags contained the logos of Chanel, Dolce & Gabbana, Fendi, La Perla, and Henri Bendel. One of the women opened the door behind the driver's seat and placed the remainder of her bags on the back seat. When she turned slightly, I caught a glimpse of her face. "Jane!"

"Jane who?"

Zack's question barely registered. My mind raced. From what I'd seen of her wardrobe so far, Jane wore strictly designer labels. Given the way Rosalie was treating her, she certainly had the right to indulge herself in more than a little retail therapy while in New Jersey. I knew nothing about Omaha, but I suspected their malls didn't rise to the level of Short Hills. Jane's college friend—who else could the other woman be?—had introduced her to a shopper's paradise for women with bulging bank accounts.

My attention fixed on Jane's companion, an exceedingly large woman. I studied her profile as she lumbered around the car to deposit the rest of her bags behind the passenger seat. Why did she look so familiar? I wracked my brain, trying to place her. Then it hit me. The octagonal, red-framed glasses. The frizzy orange hair. "Oh my god!"

SIX

"What?" asked Zack.

I ignored him, trying to wrap my mind around the implications of my discovery: Jane's companion was the hospital emergency room desk clerk. The one with a name that mocked her body: Willow Something.

I watched as both women settled into the front seat of Rosalie's car. Jane started the engine, then backed out of the parking space and headed for the exit ramp. "This makes no sense," I muttered.

"Damn right," said Zack. "What's going on?"

I opened my door. Before stepping out of the car, I said, "Long story. I'll explain over dinner."

After we had settled into a booth at the restaurant and placed our orders, I told Zack how I'd discovered Rosalie unconscious at the bottom of her basement stairs. "The hospital contacted her niece. She flew in from Omaha to care for Rosalie during her recovery, but Rosalie has been very suspicious of Jane's motives. At first, I chalked up Rosalie's paranoia to her head injury and meds, but now I'm beginning to wonder."

Logically, I could see where Willow wouldn't tell me that she knew Jane. After all, it was none of my business. "I realize hospital personnel are required to adhere to patient confidentiality laws, but don't you think it's odd Jane never mentioned that her college friend works at the hospital that treated Rosalie?"

The waiter returned with the bottle of Sauvignon Blanc Zack had ordered. We waited for him to uncork the wine and pour two glasses. Once he departed, Zack asked, "Rosalie never met Jane prior to her fall?"

"No." I explained the melodramatic family history that resulted in Rosalie's parents moving to Omaha. "Who knows which version of the story is the truth, Rosalie's or Jane's? But according to Jane, she didn't even know Rosalie was still alive until the hospital contacted her."

Zack reached into his pocket and pulled out his iPhone. "What's Jane's last name?"

"Sherman."

"What else do you know about her?"

"Not much. She's single and has lived in Omaha her entire life."

Zack began to tap the screen of his phone. "What does she do for a living?"

"Some sort of financial work where she isn't tied down to an office. She said as long as she has her laptop, she's able to work anywhere."

Zack continued to tap. "Anything else?"

"Her parents are dead. No siblings. Rosalie is her only living relative."

He stopped tapping, studied his phone, and frowned as he

began scrolling. The more he scrolled, the deeper the frown lines grew on either side of his mouth and across his forehead. Finally, he handed the phone to me. "This is the real Jane Sherman."

Zack had accessed Jane Sherman's Facebook page. My jaw dropped as I stared at the image on the screen. The real Jane Sherman bore no resemblance to the doppelganger who'd moved into Rosalie's home. "It's a common name," I said. "There could be more than one Jane Sherman in Omaha."

"Read through her profile and postings."

The information left no doubt. The real Jane Sherman was one of those clueless individuals who share far too many personal details of her life on social media. Everything the fake Jane had told me about herself was documented on the real Jane Sherman's Facebook page, including the reason for her parents' flight to Omaha. She described the aunt she'd never met as a jealous sociopath, bent on destroying the love between her mother and father.

Slowly the pieces began to slip into place. "The hospital never contacted Rosalie's niece. Jane and Willow are running a con."

"That's my guess."

Rosalie wasn't paranoid. She had every right to be suspicious of Jane because Jane wasn't Jane. "The hospital gave Jane Rosalie's purse. She had access to all of Rosalie's credit cards."

"Which she's obviously putting to good use, judging from the number of shopping bags those two crammed into the car."

"She also had plenty of time to go through Rosalie's financial records before Rosalie was discharged from the hospital." Instead of worrying about Jane pinching her quilts and knickknacks, Rosalie should have been concerned with Jane getting her hands on her bank accounts. "Should we call the police?"

"Not yet. We need proof for the police to make arrests. Jane—or whoever she is—can easily claim that Rosalie gave her the credit cards to use. And gifted her with anything else she's stolen."

"Rosalie would never do that."

"Where's your proof? It's Jane's word against the word of a medicated woman recovering from head trauma. We also don't want to tip those two off and have them move on to their next victim."

"You think they've done this before?"

"Undoubtedly. My guess is they're grifters, moving around the country, repeatedly pulling off this con. I bet the one who works at the hospital is a fairly new hire. She bides her time, waiting for the admittance of an elderly patient with no family in the area. Then they set their scheme in motion and disappear once they've wiped out their unsuspecting mark. By the time anyone's the wiser, they're long gone."

A two-ton boulder settled in the pit of my stomach. "And I played right into their hands by telling Willow about Rosalie's niece."

Zack reached across the table and clasped my hand in his. "Don't beat yourself up. She probably accessed Rosalie's records the moment the ambulance wheeled her into Emergency. You didn't tell her anything she didn't already know or wouldn't find out soon enough on her own."

I wondered how a photojournalist who spends his days tracking down endangered shrews knew about the modus operandi of grifters, but I didn't ask. There are things about Zack I've decided are best filed under the *Ignorance is Bliss* category. I already have plenty of worries keeping me awake at night.

The waiter arrived with our dinners. Over platters of Salmone al Forno for me and Gamberi alla Brace for Zack, we began formulating a plan to uncover the proof we'd need to present to the police.

Before heading home, we made a quick stop at Pottery Barn Kids where Zack bought Mia and Chloe a dollhouse expensive enough to qualify for a mortgage.

~*~

The next morning, I called Rosalie to invite her to a quilt show in Sussex County. Jane answered the phone. "I'm sure she'd love to go, but how will she get around? She can't walk more than a short distance with her casts."

"I have a wheelchair we can use." Karl had purchased one for Lucille after the accident that brought her to live with us. Given that Karl had set the *accident* in motion, it was the least he could do. I learned of the circumstances surrounding the hit-and-run that nearly killed his mother shortly after his death. I'll take that secret to my grave, not that Lucille would believe me if I told her the truth.

I gave Zack the thumbs-up. "I just hope she doesn't freak when we tell her what's going on."

"Since she already has suspicions about Jane, knowing Rosalie, she'll say, 'I told you so.'"

Zack brought the wheelchair up from the basement. After giving it a thorough cleaning, he loaded it into the trunk of my car. Then I drove around the corner to pick up Rosalie.

"Have a nice time," said Jane, holding the front door open as I maneuvered the wheelchair through the opening.

"Don't expect us back until dinnertime," I said. "What will you do with an entire day to yourself?"

She nodded over to where her laptop sat on the dining room

table. "I plan to catch up on some work."

"Have a productive day," I said.

She smiled. "I will."

I'll bet.

As I settled Rosalie into the front passenger seat of my car, she asked, "When did you and Jane arrange this outing?"

"I called half an hour ago."

"Odd that I didn't hear the phone ring."

"Maybe you were in the bathroom at the time." I placed the wheelchair in the trunk, then settled behind the wheel. After driving around the block, I pulled into my driveway.

"Did you forget something?" she asked.

I shifted in my seat to face her. "There is no quilt show, Rosalie."

"I don't understand."

"Come inside. We need to discuss something."

"Is this about Jane?"

I nodded.

"Whatever you have to say in her defense, you can save your breath. That woman is up to something. I know it."

"And you're absolutely right. I'm sorry I doubted you."

Rosalie's mouth dropped open. "You believe me?"

"I do."

"What made you change your mind?"

"My trip to the mall last night."

Her brow furrowed as she puzzled through my statement. Then she said, "I don't care if you took a trip to Jupiter as long as you finally realize I'm not crazy."

"I never thought you were crazy, Rosalie."

"Bull hockey! I could see it in your eyes. You thought I was developing dementia."

When I didn't deny the accusation, she asked, "What happened at the mall to make you change your mind?"

"Come inside. I'll explain everything."

SEVEN

Sitting between Zack and me, Rosalie stared at the image of the real Jane Sherman on my laptop screen. "I knew it!" She slammed her good fist on my kitchen table, rattling the cups of coffee I'd poured for the three of us. "I told you she was up to no good. Why are we just sitting here? We need to call the police. I want her arrested. And I need to cancel my credit cards."

"Not yet," said Zack. While Lucille showered, he'd taken Mephisto on a covert operation to spy on Jane. When I pulled out of Rosalie's driveway, Zack and Mephisto were standing a few feet from my car. Since Jane had never met Zack nor seen Mephisto, a man walking a dog along Rosalie's street would raise no suspicions.

"Did she leave the house?" I asked.

"Almost immediately after you pulled out of Rosalie's driveway."

"Which means she's probably off spending more of my money," said Rosalie. "The only way to stop her is to cancel the credit cards."

"If you do that while she's shopping, she'll know you're on to her," said Zack. "We need time to discover what else she's done."

"How?"

"We're going back to your house," I said.

"Why?"

"To check your financial records."

The color drained from Rosalie's face. "What if she's already wiped me out?"

"Let's assess the damage first," said Zack. "Then we'll call the police."

I grabbed my laptop, and we drove Rosalie back to her home. "Where do we start?" she asked after we entered the empty house.

"Can you access your bank and stock accounts online?" asked Zack.

"Yes, but I rarely do. I prefer dealing with people, when it comes to money, not machines."

"Where do you keep all your files?" I asked.

Rosalie directed me to the downstairs bedroom she used as her quilting room. "There's a file cabinet in the closet. You'll find everything in there."

"And your checkbook?"

"Top center drawer of my desk."

"What about passwords?" asked Zack.

"On a piece of paper tacked to the bulletin board above my desk."

I stifled a groan. I'd be giving Rosalie a lesson on Internet security in the near future—assuming Jane hadn't already wiped her out, thus negating the need for any passwords.

I placed my laptop on her dining room table and headed to the quilt room with Zack. Behind me I heard Rosalie sigh heavily and mutter under her breath. "I never should have let that woman in my home."

I felt like she'd plunged a dagger between my shoulder blades. "This is my fault," I said to Zack. "If I hadn't convinced Rosalie to give Jane a chance, none of this would have happened."

Zack stopped at the entrance to the quilt room, turned to face me, and placed his hands on my shoulders. "You're forgetting that the hospital gave Jane Rosalie's purse with her wallet, credit cards, and keys. Even if Rosalie refused Jane's help after she was released from the hospital, Jane already had everything she needed to run her con while Rosalie was still lying unconscious in her hospital bed."

"Is that supposed to make me feel better?"

"It's supposed to make you realize this isn't your fault. Besides, if it weren't for you spotting Jane and Willow at the mall last night, their con would continue until they'd bled Rosalie dry."

"Then Rosalie has Patricia to thank, not me."

"Patricia?"

"If she hadn't given birth to the twins, we wouldn't have gone to the mall. Chalk one up to the butterfly effect."

Zack shook his head and chuckled. Then he dropped his hands from my shoulders and headed for the closet.

While he pulled file folders of bank, brokerage, and credit card accounts, I retrieved Rosalie's checkbook and blank checks. Thumbing through each pad, checking the sequential numbering, I discovered random checks missing. "Twenty-two checks have been removed," I told Zack as he gathered the files into his arms.

I grabbed the sheet of paper with Rosalie's passwords off the bulletin board. Not only had she left her passwords in plain sight, they were all very similar.

Once we returned to the dining room Zack had no trouble logging onto Rosalie's accounts. Unfortunately, neither had Jane. We quickly discovered that over the past week she'd siphoned off nearly seventy-five thousand dollars.

"You'd think someone would have noticed the unusual activity and notified Rosalie," I said.

"They may have," said Zack.

"I never received any calls from the bank or my broker," said Rosalie.

"Jane may have intercepted the calls," he said.

Rosalie grew thoughtful. "Come to think of it, I can't remember my phone ringing at all since coming home from the hospital."

"She may have had your calls forwarded to her cell phone."

I turned to Rosalie. "That would explain why you didn't hear the phone ring when I called this morning."

She let out a string of expletives that shocked me. Except for the odd *bull hockey*, I'd never heard Rosalie utter so much as a *damn*. "Her phone is constantly ringing, and she's always excusing herself to another room before answering the calls."

The woman had thought of everything. Zack was right. She and Willow were pros.

Turning our attention to Rosalie's credit card accounts, we searched until we found her Visa and American Express passwords. When Zack logged onto the accounts, we discovered Jane had charged over thirty thousand dollars at the mall over the last few days and had already racked up over five thousand dollars in charges so far today.

Rosalie trembled with rage. "Now can we call the police?"

Zack logged off the American Express website. "We need

more," he said.

"What on earth for?" Angry tears gathered in Rosalie's eyes.

I patted her hand. "A good lawyer will argue that you gave her access to your credit cards and accounts."

"But I did no such thing!"

"I know."

The tears began to spill down her cheeks. She bowed her head and covered her eyes with her good hand. "This is a nightmare. How do I get my money back? How do we make her pay for what she's done?"

I stood up and started pacing around the dining room. What else could we do to prove the phony Jane had committed fraud? Then it hit me. "Of course!"

"What?" asked Rosalie.

Could it be that simple? I raced upstairs to the bedroom Jane was using and rummaged through the closet and dresser drawers. Nothing. I knew her laptop had to be hidden somewhere. I got down on my hands and knees and looked under the bed. Not there, either. I finally found it when I removed the quilt and began systematically poking my arms under the mattress. Returning downstairs, I placed the laptop on the dining room table. "I'll bet we'll find all the proof we need right here."

Five minutes later Zack turned to Rosalie and said, "Now we call the police."

~*~

Officers Harley and Fogarty arrived ten minutes later. "Don't you need a search warrant?" I asked after we explained the situation but before showing them the files on Phony Jane's computer. We certainly didn't want Jane and Willow—or whoever they were—getting off on a technicality due to inadmissible evidence.

"Not to take a look," said Fogarty. "By entering Mrs. Schneider's home under false pretenses, she's forfeited her rights to privacy."

"If the computer files prove incriminating, we'll need a warrant to remove the computer from the premises," added Harley. "The detective from the fraud unit will execute one."

Both officers stood behind Zack, reading over his shoulder, as he opened one file after another and slowly scrolled through them.

Harley whistled under his breath. "You'd think someone who'd devised such a sophisticated scheme would password protect her computer."

"She did," said Zack.

My jaw dropped. "You hacked your way in? In less than five minutes? Do they teach that in photojournalism school or alphabet agency school?"

He speared me with his standard I'm-not-a-spy look. "Neither. The average tech-savvy twelve-year-old would have gotten in sooner."

Right. Although it did make me wonder whether my own two sons had such skills. And if so, did I really want to know?

After looking at only a few files, Harley placed a call to a Detective Vasquez in the Union County fraud unit. "You might want to clear your schedule for this one," he said.

As Zack had suggested, the phony Jane and her sidekick had a long history of pulling this particular con throughout the country—and Phony Jane had kept meticulous records.

"So who is she, really?" I asked as we waited for the detective to arrive.

"Not sure," said Zack. "She's got dozens of aliases, not to mention scores of stolen identities. She created a database to keep them all straight."

"They could be Roma," suggested Fogarty.

"What's that?" asked Rosalie.

"The politically correct name for gypsies. They're cons have gotten more and more sophisticated over the last couple of decades."

"The fraud techs will be able to sift through everything and get to the truth," said Harley.

"I hope so," she said. "I want those women locked away for the rest of their lives."

I was about to agree when Jane walked through the front door.

EIGHT

Jane immediately zeroed in on Harley and Fogarty. "Why are the police here?"

Rosalie pointed a finger at her. "They're here to arrest you. I knew you were up to something. Now I have proof. And so do they."

Jane's gaze darted around the dining room, from Rosalie to me to Zack to the two officers. Then she zeroed in on the computer sitting in front of Zack. The color drained from her face. "Is that my computer?"

"It certainly is," said Rosalie, a smug expression filling her face. "And it's all the proof the police need to lock you up for stealing from me. And apparently from a lot of other people."

"How dare you!" Jane strode across the room and made a grab for the laptop, but Fogarty beat her to it. In one swift move his massive hand slammed down the cover and scooped up the computer.

"Step back," he ordered her.

"I will not! That's private property. You have no right to take it." She lunged at Fogarty and tried to wrestle the computer from his grip.

Harley grabbed Jane's arm in an attempt to pry her away from his partner, but Jane refused to budge. "Unless you want to add assaulting an officer to the charges that will be filed against you," he finally said, "you'll let go immediately."

Jane dropped her arms, stepped back, and switched tactics. She plastered a nervous smile on her face and waved a hand toward the computer. "This is all a huge misunderstanding," she said.

"Who are you?" demanded Rosalie.

Jane turned to face Rosalie. With a sing-song lilt to her voice, as if speaking down to a small child, she said, "I'm your niece. Jane Sherman. You know that. And I'd never steal from you, Aunt Rosalie. You're confused."

She then addressed Harley and Fogarty. "You remember how irrational she behaved the other night. This is just more of the same paranoid behavior. My aunt suffers from dementia."

"I do not!" said Rosalie.

"How does that explain the files on your computer?" I asked. "The ones that prove you're a con artist."

Jane laughed. "Con artist? Don't be silly. That's research. I'm writing a mystery novel."

Zack spoke for the first time. "Funny how there's no evidence of a novel in progress anywhere on your computer."

"That's because I'm still in the research stage. And who the hell are you?"

Rosalie didn't give Zack a chance to answer. "Why did you charge thousands of dollars to my credit cards and withdraw even more from my bank accounts? Was that also research for your book?"

Jane sighed. "Don't you remember, Aunt Rosalie? You gave me the credit cards to shop for you, and I withdrew the money to pay your hospital bills."

"Bull hockey! I did no such thing. And you're not my niece."

"Of course, I am. I'll show you my driver's license if you don't believe me." Jane walked around the table to where Rosalie sat. She reached into her purse, but instead of pulling out her wallet, she withdrew a semi-automatic pistol and pointed it at Rosalie's head.

"Now this is what's going to happen," she said, her voice growing menacing. "No one moves until I say so." With her left hand she latched onto Rosalie's right arm, the one with the hand and wrist cast, and yanked her to her feet. The dining room chair toppled backwards and crashed to the floor.

With the gun pressed against the back of Rosalie's head, Jane dragged her into the living room. "Anastasia, take the computer from the cop."

I turned to Harley and Fogarty. "Do as she says," said Harley. "We don't want anyone getting hurt."

"That's right," said Jane. "Listen to the smart cop, and no one gets hurt."

Fogarty began to hand me the laptop, but Zack reached for it. "I'll do it."

"No!" Jane waved the gun at us. "I said Anastasia. Or I start shooting."

"I'll be okay," I said to Zack as I took the computer.

"That's better," said Jane. "Now bring the laptop to me. Nice and slow."

I walked into the living room toward Jane and Rosalie. Stopping about two feet in front of them, with both hands I held out the computer. "Here."

Unless Jane sprouted a third arm, she either had to release her grip on Rosalie or put down the gun. She kept the gun pressed against Rosalie's head while she extended her left arm toward me. "Give it to me," she said.

As Jane took a step forward and reached for the computer, Rosalie swung her arm, slamming her cast hard onto Jane's wrist. The gun flew from Jane's hand, discharging as it smashed a porcelain table lamp, then ricocheted off the corner of the coffee table and skidded across the hardwood floor.

She shoved Rosalie aside and lunged for the gun. As Jane sailed past me, I swung the computer and smacked her in the back of her head. She fell forward, hitting her head on the edge of the glass-topped coffee table. While Harley, and Fogarty rushed to subdue her, Zack retrieved the gun.

Detective Vasquez pulled up to the front of the house as Harley and Fogarty were dragging a handcuffed, bloodied Jane, to their squad car.

~*~

"You could have gotten yourself killed," I told Rosalie as we waited for Detective Vasquez and his crime scene techs to bag up Jane's belongings.

"Or all of us," said Zack.

"Harley and Fogarty would have put her down before that happened," she said.

"Put her down?" We live in a town with very little crime. I doubt Harley and Fogarty have ever fired their service revolvers other than during target practice. The thought of bullets flying across Rosalie's living room sent shudders skittering up my spine.

"That is what it's called, isn't it? Besides, someone had to do something. You were all just standing there."

"We were trying to keep her from putting a bullet through your skull," said Zack.

"And I appreciate that, but the situation called for action. So I took matters into my own hands and acted."

Rosalie was either the bravest woman I'd ever met or the most reckless. Either way, she was one feisty octogenarian.

~*~

Until we knew that the police had Willow in custody, I didn't want Rosalie staying in her house. I suggested she spend the night in my home. With the boys still away, she could sleep in their room and wouldn't have to share a room with Lucille. Rosalie immediately accepted my offer. I think she, too, was afraid Willow might come after her, seeking revenge.

Harley and Fogarty stopped by after dinner to give us an update.

"She refused to talk," said Harley, "other than to demand a lawyer."

"And Willow?" I asked.

"Behind bars as well," said Fogarty, "and also not talking."

"We were able to track her down using the other one's cell phone," said Harley. "They were sharing an apartment in Millburn."

"Do you have any idea who they are?" I asked.

Harley nodded. "Turns out there are dozens of outstanding warrants from all over the country for those two. In a matter of minutes Vasquez had a hit from the FBI database."

"Jane's real name is Virginia Mayer," said Fogarty. "Willow's her older sister Deborah."

"How did they get away with it for so long?" asked Zack.

"You'd think the FBI would have notified hospitals across the country to be on the lookout for them."

"Especially Willow—Deborah," I said. "She doesn't exactly blend into the woodwork with that wild orange hair."

"According to Vasquez, Deborah Mayer is a master of disguise. They found all sorts of wigs and theatrical prosthetics in the apartment when they raided it. Every time the women moved to another part of the country, she changed her looks."

"And no one knew to keep an eye out for Virginia Mayer," added Harley, "because she never applied for a job at the hospitals."

"You were right about them." I said to Zack. "How did you know?"

He shrugged. "Years of reading mysteries and thrillers on all those intercontinental plane rides."

Or years of working for Spies R Us? I might as well give up. He'd never come clean to me.

"Jane—Virginia—was frighteningly good," I said.

"Good?" asked Rosalie. "There was nothing good about that woman."

"I mean in the way she'd perfected her act. She was totally convincing, prepared for every contingency. She never skipped a beat, never faltered. The woman had answers to questions before we even asked them. Like the pills. And the excuse about the dentist."

"She was drugging me," said Rosalie, "no matter what she claims."

"Probably," said Zack. "Keeping you confused made it easy for her to convince others of your unreliable memory."

"But more than that, she had an uncanny knack for

improvisation," I said. "She never showed any signs of hesitation or fear until she saw us with her computer."

"I'm not surprised," said Harley. "Vasquez said both women had gone to acting school. They started running cons after they failed to break into the movies."

"Maybe they gave up too soon," I said. "Virginia certainly gave an Oscar-worthy performance."

"Anyway," said Fogarty, "those two are going away for a long time." He turned to Rosalie. "You don't have to worry about them."

"What about the money they stole from me?" she asked.

He grinned. "Saved the best part for last. We recovered all of it. You'll get it back shortly. As well as all the merchandise they bought with your credit cards."

"And what am I supposed to do with all that high-priced designer crap?"

"Return it," said Fogarty.

Rosalie frowned at the casts on her arm and leg. Her eyes welled up with tears, and her voice took on a whine. "How am I supposed to do that? Most stores now have limited return policies. By the time these casts come off, it could be too late."

I looked at Zack.

His mouth quirked as he shrugged and nodded in resignation.

"Don't worry," I told Rosalie. "Zack and I will return everything for you."

Her face brightened, her eyes cleared, and she smiled. With not a trace of whine left in her voice, she said, "Thank you, Anastasia. I knew I could count on you."

And I knew I'd just been conned.

ABOUT THE AUTHOR

USA Today and Amazon bestselling and award-winning author Lois Winston writes mystery, romance, romantic suspense, chick lit, women's fiction, children's chapter books, and nonfiction. *Kirkus Reviews* dubbed her critically acclaimed Anastasia Pollack Crafting Mystery series, "North Jersey's more mature answer to Stephanie Plum." In addition, Lois is an award-winning craft and needlework designer who often draws much of her source material for both her characters and plots from her experiences in the crafts industry. Learn more about Lois and her books and sign up for her newsletter at www.loiswinston.com.